Bombshell

Second Edition

Bombshell

Second Edition

Mike Faricy

Library of Congress Control Number: 2023913835
paperback ISBN: 9798988684770
e-book ISBN: 9798988684787

MJF Publishing books may be purchased for education, Business, or promotional use. For information on bulk purchases,
please contact the author directly at mikefaricyauthor@gmail.com

Published by

MJF Publishing
https://www.mikefaricybooks.com

To Teresa

*"No, we're not going out,
I want you to myself."*

Acknowledgments

I would like to thank the following people for their help and support:

Special thanks to my editors, Kitty, Donna and Rhonda for their hard work, cheerful patience and positive feedback.

I would like to thank Ann and Julie for their creative talent and not slitting their wrists or jumping off the high bridge when dealing with my Neanderthal computer capabilities.

Special thanks to Ann for her patience.

Last, I would like to thank family and friends for their encouragement and unqualified support. Special thanks to Maggie, Jed, Schatz, Pat, Av, Emily and Pat for not rolling their eyes, at least when I was there, and most of all, to my wife Teresa whose belief, support and inspiration has from day one, never waned.

One

With all the music thumping in the place, I had to lean halfway across the bar just to give my drink order. "I'll have a pint of Summit and a Cosmopolitan," I said. The bartender nodded, maybe gave a slight sigh, I wasn't sure.

"That Cosmo for you?" the woman next to me asked, then yelled across to the bartender, "Two Summits."

She stood about five-three, brown hair, glasses, very nice figure. She had on really tight little shorts over black hose patterned to look like slinky nylons and a garter belt.

"Do I look like the Cosmo type?"

"Yeah, I knew it as soon as I saw you. You're probably a big 'Sex in the City' fan. I'm Justine," she said and held out her hand.

"Dev."

Her eyes bored into me as I shook her hand. The music fired up again, so loud we had to speak into each other's ear. We were in danger of getting body slammed by a half dozen twenty-something girls jumping up and down behind us. They were shaking their hair, waving their hands over their heads and screaming "woo, woo," as they twirled around.

"You come here often? You don't really look the type," she half-shouted.

"Woo, woo," the girls screamed, oblivious to all but themselves.

"I've managed to avoid this place thus far. Not exactly my style. I knew I was in trouble as soon as I had to pay the cover charge at the door."

She nodded toward my beer and the Cosmopolitan landing in front of me. I handed the bartender a couple of fives.

"Twelve-fifty." He seemed to smile at the joke.

"Twelve?"

"Twelve-fifty," he smiled again.

I gave him another five and shook my head.

"Apparently she's got expensive tastes. Maybe you should think about finding a girl who likes beer."

"Fortunately, she has some good points, too," I said into her ear.

"Don't we all," she said and gave me that stare again.

I raised my pint glass in a toast to Justine, knocked a couple of inches off the top, and carefully picked up the Cosmopolitan.

"Be good," I said.

"I have a lot more fun when I'm bad."

"You're telling me." I thought it might be a wise idea to retreat to my table.

I delivered the Cosmopolitan to my date, Carol. She was nestled into a gang of girlfriends, all talking about stars whose names I didn't recognize. Each one held a different colored, overpriced drink in front of them. I reached over the shoulder of some long-haired guy who had taken up residence on my stool and handed Carol her Cosmopolitan.

"Watch out, Dev, you almost spilled," she snapped. She turned, shook her head, and rolled her eyes at the guy on my stool. He smiled back at her, gave his head a shake to send his hair back over his shoulders, then used a finger to push misbehaving strands behind each ear.

"Dev, this is Nicholas, he's from France," Carol yelled over the noise.

I nodded and figured Nicholas was attracted to Carol by the same things that had attracted me.

"Dev, get Nicholas a drink, will you? What are you drinking?" Carol screamed then placed a hand on his wrist just as the music stopped.

"There is French beer, no?" Nicholas said, looking up at me hopefully.

"I don't think so."

"No Caracole? No Saxo?" He sounded put out.

"No. Just, Summit, Leinenkugel, Grain Belt and they got Guinness.

"Pity. French beer is the very best," Nicholas directed this toward Carol.

Carol smiled like she understood, like it was a fact everyone automatically knew, nodding as if she had a refrigerator full of French beer in her kitchen.

"Oh, I just love your dreamy accent. Maybe you'd like a Cosmopolitan, here try a sip of mine," she said and offered up her eight dollar drink.

"I think I may try the martini, yes?" he said, suggesting he'd never had one before.

"That sounds so cute."

"A martini?" I figured that would be at least six bucks.

"Yes, a vodka martini, a double." He suddenly sounded like he may have ordered one before.

"A double?" I asked.

"Where are the olives from?"

"The olives? A jar." I was liking Nicholas less with every passing second.

"Dev, stop it. Just go and get Nicholas his martini." Carol glared, and then graced Nicholas with her smile.

"And two olives," Nicholas reminded, holding up two fingers.

Carol gave me her look that said, '*Don't even think of causing a scene,*' then turned back to focus on Nicholas.

"Double vodka martini, your cheapest bar pour. I better have another Summit, too," I said to the bartender.

"She's onto martinis now?"

It was Justine again. Actually, I was glad to see her.

"No, some jackass took my stool, and somehow, I end up buying him a drink, a French guy."

Justine looked over my shoulder and took a long sip from her beer. As she moved to say something in my ear, she brushed against me.

"That guy with the long hair and the big ears?"

I hadn't noticed the ears, but now that she mentioned it ."Yeah, the guy with his back to us."

"He's chatting up the girl in the red?"

"Yeah, the one with the dreamy look on her face."

"I'm guessing those aren't her God-given attributes."

"You can tell that from across the room?"

"Hello, yes. God, they're fakes," she said and shook her head.

"Yeah, they are, but that never really bothered me."

"Twelve-fifty," the bartender said, setting Nicholas's martini and my beer down in front of me.

I handed him a twenty. The look on my face must have given me away.

"Just isn't shaping up to be your night, is it, Cosmo?"

"Not exactly. Can you stay put for a minute while I deliver this to Pepe Le Pew over there?"

"Yeah, promise you won't be long."

"Not a problem, believe me."

"Merci," Nicholas said, quickly grabbing the drink out of my hand then returning to Carol's charm.

"Be careful, Dev. God, you'll spill again. Did he get any on you, Nicholas?" Carol said.

I could only hope, but didn't wait for an answer and wandered back to Justine at the bar.

"So how long are they here?"

"Actually, she's with me, so—"

"I got a beer says no way."

"What?" I gave a shrug, then turned to look at Carol. She was laughing, stroking Nicholas's arm. She saw me, raised her almost empty glass, signaling for another Cosmopolitan.

"Whoa, better get on that," Justine said.

"Maybe not just yet. You here alone?"

"More or less." She glanced over her shoulder toward a group of women dancing. One of the women wore a white veil and a sign around her neck that read 'Child Bride.' She was twirling round and round in the center of the group. None of them seemed to be feeling any pain.

"So, what do you do?"

"I'm a medical assistant by day. But at night, I'm a derby Bombshell, baby." She cocked her hip, struck a pose, and fluttered her eyes at me.

"Huh?"

"Roller derby, I skate with the Bombshells."

"You're kidding."

"No, it's really fun. Don't tell me you didn't notice I was a Bombshell? What do you do?"

"You mean when I'm not getting drinks for jerks? I'm a PI."

"PI?"

"Private Investigator."

"You mean like a detective, like in the movies or CSI?"

"Yeah, exactly, only about a thousand times duller."

"Do you carry a gun?"

"Sometimes."

"Can I see it?"

"Fortunately, I left it at home. Otherwise, I would have blown my brains out about three minutes after coming into this place."

"You know, do you have a card? We might have a need for your services."

I dug a card out of my wallet and handed it to her.

"Devlin Haskell, Private Investigator," she read.

"That's me."

"So you find people and stuff, solve mysteries and crimes?"

"Sometimes. Like I said, it's a lot more boring than the movies."

"Think you'll be able to find your date?"

"What?" I turned to look at the two empty stools where Carol and Nicholas had been sitting. I couldn't spot them out on the dance floor. I guessed they'd wandered back into the crowd somewhere.

"You might be able to catch them if you hurry. I think they were headed for the back door."

“Catch them? I got a better idea. I think I owe you a beer if I recall.”

“You do.”

TWO

I was sitting in Nina's, nursing a coffee, watching the early morning crowd squirt a sugar substitute into their lattes and cappuccinos. Aaron LaZelle, a lieutenant in vice with St. Paul's finest, sat across from me. I decided to speak my mind.

"You know, with you making the exorbitant amount you do as a senior member of the police force, you'd think you could at least spring for coffee. I'm a taxpayer, after all."

"Do we really want to get into the taxes you pay? I know a few IRS guys, this time of year, they got a little time on their hands. They could check into it, do an audit or two, you know, make sure you're not paying more than your fair share." He looked around, stared at an attractive dark-haired woman in tight jeans and a T-shirt waiting in line to place an order.

"On second thought, thanks, but no thanks. Like your caramel roll?"

"Always," he replied.

"You know anything about women's roller derby?"

"You mean where they skate round and round with jams and jammers? They've got those great names and look really hot."

"Clearly, you know more than me."

"Actually, I don't. It's been years since I was at one of those. Pretty fun if I recall. I think they actually do a lot of charity work."

"Charity work, like praying and stuff?" I said.

"Yeah, that's right, Dev, they conduct a prayer service. No they fundraise, donate a lot to food banks, maybe a kids program, the kind of stuff you'd be really involved in." He shook his head, looking back at the same dark-haired woman. She'd moved forward in line a couple of spaces.

"I like kids and shit."

"Yeah, sure you do. Admit it, you like the mommies."

"Well yeah, that too."

"Are you doing something with roller derby? No offense, but couldn't most of them kick the hell out of you?"

I ignored his comment. "I met a girl last night. She does it, roller derby I mean. Seemed like a nice girl."

"Well, then she won't be interested in you. If she was so nice, what was she doing in one of the sleazy joints you frequent?"

"God, it was the Dew Drop. I still haven't gotten my hearing back."

"What were you doing in that place?"

"Wasting time and money. You know you have to pay a cover charge just to get into that place so you can spend more money on overpriced, bullshit drinks?"

"Yeah, I'd guess you were a little bit out of your usual demographic, but once inside, you got to hang with the beautiful people."

"I think I was one of the few straight guys in there."

"Not surprising. Excuse me for a minute," he said. Then he stood up and walked over to the counter just as the dark-haired woman was picking up her coffee.

"Kristi." I heard him call, but then couldn't hear anything else. The look on her face suggested Aaron might be saying something a little more official than hello. They stepped outside. I could see her through the front window standing on the sidewalk, nodding, then shaking her head and nodding again. She suddenly leaned forward and gave him a kiss on the cheek, nodded a few more times, waved, and walked down the street. Aaron watched her for a long moment before he strolled back in.

"Business?" I asked.

"Manner of speaking," he said, then stuffed the last of the caramel roll into his mouth and licked the tip of his thumb and forefinger.

"She a working girl?"

"Sign of the times. Architect by training, escort by necessity. She's a nice kid. I played hockey with a couple of her brothers."

"So, are you checking her pricing or what?"

He shook his head and glanced around the room.

"No, just told her we got a sting coming up, working the Internet, told her to watch out and be careful."

"When does it start?"

"It doesn't. Nothing like that in the works. The only thing we got coming up is more budget cuts."

"So why'd you tell her—"

"It's kind of like pulling someone over for speeding. Everyone else slows down. Same deal, I'm just reminding her to be careful. You know how much architectural work is out there right now? Zero."

"So she's got an online ad?"

"An ad? No, a website that takes credit cards. They all do. That's the business model now. You were telling me about the Dew Drop."

"Yeah, you remember Carol?"

"Is she the Kindergarten teacher?"

"Kindergarten? No, that chick dropped me six months ago. Carol does something with the State. I forget exactly what. I can never remember the department. Anyway, we went there to the Dew Drop to meet some of her pals." I went on to tell Aaron about the noise, the dancing, Carol leaving with the French guy, Nicholas, and me meeting Justine at the bar.

"Sounds perfect. Carol dumps you, and you meet someone else before she's out the door. You are a real piece of work, buddy."

"Yeah, well anyway, I'm gonna give this Justine a call. And, I should probably play the wounded lover with Carol…try for a final sympathy roll in the sack."

"God knows that opportunity doesn't happen too often in your life."

"Actually, I think this could be a first."

I walked the half-block back home from Nina's. On my way, I called Carol, ready to play on her sympathies, tell her how heart-broken I was.

"Bon Jour, I'm unable to take your call just now. Please leave a message, Merci."

I didn't mean to leave a sigh as my message on her cell, it just came out that way. She was already learning French? I'll give you some Merci, I thought, then climbed in the car and drove to my office.

I had three days worth of verifying job references for a small company staring me in the face. Times being what they were, the company was overwhelmed with applications from qualified people. My job was to check out employment histories and references. It amounted to a lot of drudgery, and absolutely no romance, just like my life at the moment.

I'd been looking out the office window for maybe forty-five minutes, staring at St. Kate's coeds, waiting for the bus, and watching people dash into The Spot for lunch. A liquid lunch. The Spot didn't serve food. I was telling myself I should do the same when my phone rang.

I put on my best 'feeling down' voice and answered.

"Haskell Investigations," I said. I pictured Carol pacing back and forth in the hallway of some State building, embarrassed, afraid of what I might say. She'd probably spent the better part of the morning working up the courage to call me, wondering if I'd hang up as soon as I heard her voice.

"Hi Dev, Justine. You know from last night. Are you free to talk?"

"Justine? No, I mean yes, yeah."

"You sure? I don't want to interrupt."

"Nothing that can't wait."

Outside, the Randolph Avenue bus had just pulled away. It would be at least twenty-five minutes before any more women would be waiting on the corner. On my desk, I had a mountain of boring applications and references to wade through. I had time, plenty of time.

"Okay, just as long as you're sure."

"Yeah, nice to hear your voice. I was going to give you a call and see if you wanted to get together."

"Well, actually, that's maybe why I'm calling. I mean, I made some team calls this morning. We'd like to talk with you, see if we could hire you for a security gig. That is if you've got the time. I'm really sorry, but it's on pretty short notice. We'd need you in two days. For maybe a day and a half, tops."

I looked at the pile of job applications I had yet to verify. I stared at the two darts embedded in the wall a couple of inches to the right of my dartboard. The mailman had already come and gone, leaving nothing for me

except a grocery store circular, and some credit card offer I knew would be rejected the moment I sent it in.

"In two days? I could probably adjust some things.
I'd have to make a couple of phone calls, put a number
of people off and reschedule."

"You sure? I mean, we were hoping we could sit
down with you tonight, go over some stuff. I'm sorry this
is all coming up so fast."

"Tonight? I think that could work. I'll make it work.
You tell me where and when. Let me make some calls,
and I'll get back to you this afternoon if there's a problem."

"You sure? I don't want to—"

"Justine, I'm moving you up to the top of the list.
Can I call you back this afternoon?"

"I really appreciate it. Thanks, Dev," she said and
hung up.

I wandered over to The Spot to celebrate with a liquid lunch.

Three

There were five of them sitting around the table when I arrived, teammates from the Bombshells all drinking beer. Not a Cosmopolitan in sight. Justine introduced them using their roller derby names.

"Helen Killer, Maiden Bed, Brandi Manhattan and Cheatin Hart," she said.

Each woman nodded at me as Justine pointed. They were all attractive, very attractive. I had the feeling I was about to land the cakewalk job of all time.

"Nice to meet you, ladies. Justine, I don't think you ever told me your Derby name."

"Spankie," a chorus trumpeted back.

"Really? Ladies, just call me Dev. So, Justine, I mean, Spankie mentioned you had a need for my services."

"We've got the Hasting Hustlers coming in on Thursday, and there have been problems wherever they go."

"Hastings, you mean the town eight miles down-river from St. Paul?" I asked.

"No, not really. More like the town in England, where the Battle of Hastings took place in ten-sixty-six,

Harold the Second and William of Normandy. It changed British History. Well, and the rest of Western Europe."

I think it was Maiden Bed, who just gave me the school lesson, but maybe I was mixing her up with Cheatin Hart. I suddenly couldn't remember names. Well, except for Spankie.

"Define 'problems wherever they go,'" I said, thinking some sexy creature with a nickname like Nasty Nicki or Lotta Luv, and I was going to get paid to watch them while they showered.

"Their big name star is Harlotte Davidson," Helen Killer said. I remembered her name because she was the first girl introduced to me.

"Big draw," someone said.

"Huge," one of the other girls added.

"We're lucky to get them in here. It'll just about make our year with this one bout. Anyway, one of the things they require in the contract is security."

"Security?" I asked, thinking it might make a lot of sense to be with Harlotte in the shower room.

"She's had some stalker idiot after her for almost a year now."

"Stalker?" I said.

Nods all around the table.

"What does he do, hang around in the hotel? Try and get into the locker room and leave her love letters or take naked photos?"

"If only," Justine said.

"Spankie?" I asked.

She shook her head then seemed to shudder almost imperceptibly.

"Well, he mailed a couple of fingers."

"Fingers?" I half-shouted.

"Then, you guys remember? He slipped that one under her door?" I thought Brandi Manhattan said that.

"That was down in Chicago," Justine added.

"Has anyone contacted the police?"

"Here?"

I nodded.

"Yeah, we got the usual. We can pay one of their off duty guys to hang around outside the door, things like that. They said they'd keep an eye out, but there isn't much they can do. I mean, most of it has come through the mail. Not like there was a return address you could drive over to and ask some jerk what the hell he was thinking."

"Except for Chicago, when it was slipped under the door."

"Fingers?" I asked again.

"Yeah, and always the middle one, like he's giving her the finger or something."

"Creepy," Helen Killer chimed in.

"Does she have security? Someone with the team, someone keeping an eye on things."

"Yeah, but they want us to provide someone local. I mean I get it, it makes sense. Their guy can watch Harlotte. He'll know the practice routine, the hotel, all the usual, but he's not a local guy."

I was still stuck a few paces back, thinking fingers? What the hell?

"Fingers, and always the middle one?"

Nods all around.

"This happened more than twice?"

More nods.

"I think two through the mail, then Chicago," Justine said.

"So I'd just follow her around, with the Hustlers' security, that it?"

"Maybe, you tell us, you're the Private Investigator. What would you normally do?"

"I'd just follow her around, with the Hustlers' security." I detected a slight widening of their eyes, so I embellished. "Work as the local interface with the police. I know most of the key players on the police force. I'd want to coordinate with the Hastings Hustlers security folks about what they've been doing thus far. Find out what they're worried about, deal with any of their immediate concerns."

"Worried about? They're worried about some nut case sending human fingers through the mail and finally getting bold enough to slip one under the door. I mean, right under the damn door. That's what they're worried about."

"Yeah, I get that. But are they worried the same guy is going to take a shot at her during the bout? Where do you skate? Are there metal detectors? Is this finger deal just centered on their star attraction, Harlotte? Did she or any of her teammates receive threatening letters or phone calls? Look, we can sit here all night and go over what we might do, might not do, and at the end of the night, we could be completely wrong," I said.

"So, now what?" Justine asked.

"I'd like to contact these people, talk to them before they arrive, maybe get some things lined up in advance. The better prepared we are, the better off everyone will be. You got a phone number where I could reach them?"

"I can have that information for you tomorrow morning," Justine said.

Four

Her condo was on the fourth floor of a five-story building-red brick Victorian place with gargoyles, black trim, stained glass, and gables, built in eighteen-eighty. It was the perfect place for a Halloween party.

"You want a beer or something stronger?" Justine asked.

She kicked off her shoes at the door, tossed her purse on a black leather couch, one of two sitting perpendicular to a fireplace with a glass-topped coffee table between them. The room was long with a three-panel bay window at the far end and a stained glass window above that with some kind of flower pattern. The street lights from four stories down cast colored reflections across her living room ceiling.

"Beer's just fine for me."

A hallway ran straight ahead along the length of the condo, exposed brick on one side and doors to various rooms on the other. Track lighting along the ceiling lit the hall and highlighted three framed paintings hung on the brick wall. The paintings were roller derby scenes. Girls skating around a banked track wearing hot pants, you could feel a sense of speed and action just by looking at the things, the paintings.

"You do these?" I asked, staring briefly at the paintings before following her into the kitchen at the far end of the hall.

"No, some California guy. That's me in them, in the purple jersey. He did ten of the things if you can believe it, gave me a deal. He had a show and everything. I guess it went pretty well." Her voice was muffled as she bent over and reached into a gigantic refrigerator.

"Here's to you," she said and handed me a bottle.

A few beers later, we ended up on one of the couches, legs resting across the coffee table. A couple of table lamps with stained glass dragonflies on the shades dimly lit the room. Light from the lamps reflected off the glazed fireplace tiles.

"You think there'll be any trouble?" she asked.

"You mean with Harlotte Davidson and the fingers?"

"No, I mean because I'm almost out of beer, yes with Harlotte and the fingers."

"I hope not. I don't think there will be. But, I'll give you this, it's pretty damn strange."

"Yeah, and not the kind of publicity we're looking for."

"I don't know. You could probably get a sellout crowd showing up just to see if anything was going to happen. People dig this weird shit. Look at all the folks into the whole vampire thing," I said, then sipped.

"That is so not the type of fans we're looking for. We've worked really hard to get beyond the image of strippers on roller skates, and then something like this comes along."

"Maybe it's someone who gets their kicks getting headlines. You know, their fifteen minutes of fame. If that doesn't happen, if you keep it quiet, maybe the guy will just go away."

"Or get more aggressive," she said.

"There is that."

"Who would let some guy cut off their finger?" she said, then shuddered, swallowing her beer.

"I've been thinking about that. At first, I was thinking, it's him, you know some nut case doing it to himself, but there are too many middle fingers for one guy. Then, I thought maybe homeless people, druggies, but that seems rather far fetched. I'm guessing someone with ready access."

"Ready access? To fingers? You gotta be kidding. How does that work?" she said and shuddered.

"Maybe it's someone who works in a hospital, a morgue, or a funeral home, something along those lines."

"Oh, that's comforting."

"Just thinking out loud."

"You hear back from Miss Cosmopolitan?" she asked, moving quickly away from the subject of fingers.

"No, tell you the truth I'm not really interested, I guess." I saw no benefit admitting I heard Carol's stupid

French phone message. I could only hope little old Nicholas was just that, little.

"Need a hug?"

"What?"

"Get over here, stupid," she said and took her glasses off.

Five

Justine pushed her card next to my coffee cup. It was almost six in the morning, and if I was going to be up at this hour, I was in desperate need of coffee, and lots of it. She was already dressed in blue hospital scrubs, doing something to her eyes using a brush and a mirror while she sat at her kitchen counter. "I wrote the Hustlers' phone number on the back of my card. Here. Jimmy McNaughton is the manager's name. If he's not the guy to talk to, he'll know who is. He's a little hard to understand. You know, the accent."

"I'll give him a call this morning. Are they flying in tomorrow?"

She glanced over at me.

"No, they're on a team bus, coming out of Denver. They're probably west of Omaha right about now, somewhere in the middle of Nebraska."

"Gee, the romance of show biz."

"Denver's a nice town."

"I wasn't referring to Denver."

"Oh yeah, that. We should be looking pretty good to them by the time they get up here. I just hope everything goes okay and nothing happens while they're in town."

"I'll make sure nothing happens."

"Let's hope," she said.

It was almost noon before I reached Jimmy McNaughton on his phone. I'd spent the morning forcing myself to work through the stack of job applications. Between Jimmy's accent and phone coverage in the middle of Nebraska, I could only make out about every third word he said. But I got the gist of it. He gave me the name of their hotel, when they expected to arrive, and then casually added, "Looking forward to meeting you, mate. Had another little surprise waiting for us last night."

"A surprise?"

"Taped to the door of the bus. An envelope addressed to Harlotte with another bloke's finger inside."

"She okay?"

"Didn't want to bother her about it."

"What'd Denver police say?"

"Didn't care to wait to tell you the truth. The girls have a schedule to keep. We'd lose a day waiting for them to tell us I was right and it was a finger. You'd think your man would be running out of mates at this point."

"How many does that make?"

"Four, that we know of."

"All the middle finger?"

"Right."

"You said four, you know of, you think there may be more than that?"

"I'm not sure what to think."

"Let me do some checking on this end. I'll be waiting for you at the hotel."

"Cheers," Jimmy said and hung up.

"Homicide," the voice answered three minutes later.

"Detective Manning," I said, against my better judgment.

"Who's calling?"

"Devlin Haskell," I said, knowing this was bound to slow things up.

"Just a minute."

It wasn't a minute, or two or even three. I waited for close to ten and was just about to hang up when he graced me with his voice.

"Manning."

"Detective Manning, Devlin Haskell."

"Oh, damn it, it's actually you calling. I thought they said someone was calling you in, DOA. My mistake," he said, then cracked the ever-present piece of gum into the phone.

"Sorry to ruin your day, Detective."

"I'm used to it," he said, not joking.

"Say, I just wanted to touch base with you. I'm providing security for an individual and she—"

"Security? You? She must be nuts."

I ignored his comment.

"She's been receiving threats for some time. The thing's escalated to some nut case mailing her human fingers. She started receiving—"

"This that English roller derby broad, Harlotte Davidson?"

"Yeah, as a matter of fact."

"They're heading our way from Denver?"

"Yeah."

"We're aware of it."

"What are you doing about it?"

"Doing about it?"

"Yeah, is there a plan, are you putting extra people on?"

"Extra people? Have you read the damn newspapers or turned off the cartoons and watched the news in the last couple of years? We're down by almost fifteen percent. Put some people on, gee, why didn't I think of that? Tell you what, I'll just walk over to the squad room, you know, find a-half-dozen guys who are sitting around eating doughnuts and tell them to stand by. In fact, good thing you called, now you can tell them here. Hang on a minute, just let me put you on speakerphone."

"I'll take that as a no, there isn't a plan."

"A plan, yeah, I got a plan. We're watching every post office. One of those envelopes comes in with no return address, we'll be the first to let you know."

"They weren't all mailed, the fingers."

"You referring to Chicago where the guy slipped it under the door of the hotel room?"

"Not just Chicago, Detective."

"You mean the envelope taped to the door of the bus in Denver last night? Checked out like all the others."

"Have you guys thought of maybe running the fingerprint on the thing? I mean, does it strike you as strange you got four people missing a finger and no one has reported an assault or a body or a missing person or anything?"

"Wow, Sherlock, amazing you aren't a cop with all those great ideas you have. Yeah, I think the various departments thought about running the fingerprint. Just one problem…there isn't one."

"Isn't one?"

"The finger print, it's missing. Whoever's doing this cuts off the finger tip. Anything else you care to add? Pardon the pun." Manning chuckled at his humor.

"Do you have a plan?" I asked again, not sounding too sure.

"A plan? Yeah, I got a plan. Hope nothing happens here and that they're all out of our jurisdiction sooner rather than later. How's that sound to you, Haskell?"

"Sounds like a plan, Detective."

"Always a pleasure," he said, and hung up.

Six

Jimmy McNaughton and the Hastings Hustlers arrived about seven that night. They looked like you'd expect after riding on a bus for a thousand hours from Denver up to St. Paul, tired and cranky.

"Right, the girls will check in, then meet in the lobby in an hour or so. I'd say that gives us just enough time to get acquainted over a pint. Lead on, mate," Jimmy said, fleeing the check-in scene in the lobby and sounding like he could use a break from the ladies.

"Two more, please." Jimmy signaled to the bartender twenty minutes later. He followed her every step of the way with his eyes as she walked down the bar toward the beer taps. I had a feeling he and I were going to get along just fine.

"You were telling me about your plans, what you've been doing with Harlotte."

"What we've been doing," he said, turning back to me and running a hand over his shaved head. "Is just running a bit of interference. About all we can do, we've got her ring-fenced. There's another girl who shares the room with her, a black belt in karate. We check the mail. We'll post someone from the hotel staff outside her door the entire time we're here. I'll escort her to and from the track. If she does an interview, I'll be there standing next to her. We scrutinize everyone who's going to be near her. Hell, we'll even check her meals before they're placed in front of her."

"How's she holding up?"

"Harlotte? Pretty well. Don't let the name fool you. She's the strong silent type."

I grinned.

"No, really, she is. The girls go out, Harlotte is the one in the corner drinking a coke. She might order a white wine if she was really going to celebrate, but it would take her all night to finish a glass. She calls home every night, talks to the kids and her husband for ten minutes."

"We talking about the same Harlotte Davidson?"

"Husband's a primary school teacher. That's show-biz," Jimmy said.

He wasn't kidding. Another pint later, we were joined by Harlotte and a raven-haired beauty introduced as Emma Babe. Emma was Harlotte's black belt room-mate.

"A black belt in Karate and Tai Kwan Do," she informed me. I sensed it was warning, suggesting she'd have no problem kicking my butt. I turned my attention to Harlotte.

"Fiona Simmons," she said, holding out her hand.

"Devlin Haskell."

If she was wearing makeup, it wasn't much. She was attractive, but not in the drop dead, knockout way I had expected. Her long blonde hair was pulled back tightly in a ponytail. She seemed to have a nice figure, dressed in jeans and hidden beneath a bulky sweatshirt that read St. Margaret's School for Girls.

"Dev is going to make sure things continue running smoothly while we're here in St Paul's," Jimmy said.

"St. Paul," I corrected. "We have an inferiority complex with a larger city like Minneapolis right next door."

They nodded in unison.

"It sounds like everything Jimmy has been doing is working, so we're not going to change anything. I've been in touch with our police force. They're aware of your situation. We'll just keep a low profile. Your bout is tomorrow night, and then you're leaving the following morning as I understand it."

"Actually, leaving right after the bout. It will be after midnight by the time we're loaded. Drive down to Chicago, and then the team skates that night."

"Not much time for a rest," I said.

"There appears to have been a lack of appreciation for the distances you have over here when the schedule was arranged," Jimmy said.

"Driving from Denver, the deforestation we saw was absolutely amazing," Emma added.

"Deforestation?"

"Not a tree in sight for as far as the eye could see. I guessed they were all cut down for your log cabins. We all took pictures out the bus window, American greed." She looked very satisfied with the analogy.

"You drove across the great plains. That's what you saw." I said.

Blank looks all around.

"There never were any trees. That was the part of the country you see in the old cowboy movies, buffalo, rolling hills, Indians. People literally went insane out there from the wind blowing constantly."

Emma looked at me in a way that suggested the insanity probably continued for generations.

"Fiona, do you mind if I ask you a couple of questions about this stalker business?"

She looked at Jimmy for a moment, and he nodded.

"Go ahead," she said.

"Any idea who or why?"

She shook her head, but seemed to think for a bit. "No idea whatsoever. I thought we had crazies back home, but this is like something a footballer would think up."

"Footballer, what we'd call soccer over here?" I said.

"Yes. They're fanatic, you know? But this, for us, me? It just doesn't make any sense."

"So it began when you came over here? It didn't follow you over?"

"Nothing until we were in the states. The first one was in St. Louis?" She looked at Jimmy for confirmation.

"St. Louis, it was actually waiting for us at the hotel. The envelope, that is."

"Then Kansas City, Chicago. That was the one pressed under the door, Chicago, and that's it."

I didn't mention Denver. Jimmy had said he didn't want to upset her.

"Have you had any interaction with fans here? A disagreement, perceived slight, something like that?"

Both women shook their heads 'no.'

"Nothing. Everyone has been really, really nice. Unfortunately, since this started, we've really been kept apart, no more autographs. We used to do photo sessions for all the kids. That's been stopped. Not sure what good it's done to tell you the truth."

"God forbid we'd be able to go out for a pint or meet a lad. Poor Fiona can't go to the loo without someone holding her hand," Emma said.

"Just playing the odds, being careful, darling," Jimmy said.

"I know, but it's such a shame. One plonker can ruin the whole thing for everyone…doesn't seem quite fair." Emma looked at me, sized me up for the obvious plonker I was.

"It's not fair," I said. "But right now, everyone is more concerned with you and your teammates staying safe while you're in our fair city. You need anything you let me know. I'll be working with Jimmy. You may not see me, but I'll be there," I said.

"Too many American movies, you ask me," Emma added.

"I'll even watch out for you," I said to Emma.

"I can see to me-self," she said and stood. Fiona followed.

"Back to the room then ladies?" Jimmy asked, but with a tone that suggested a little more.

They both nodded.

"Pleasure to meet you, Mr. Haskell," Fiona said.

"Please, call me Dev. I'll see you around."

She smiled, then caught up with Emma already at the door.

"She seems like a nice woman," I said.

"Emma?" Jimmy looked at me.

"Fiona."

"I could tell Emma had a soft spot for you," he said and smiled.

"If that was her way of being nice, I'd hate to be on her bad side."

Jimmy nodded.

Seven

I phoned Justine on my way home.

"Hello."

"Spankie?"

"Hey, how'd it go?"

"Nice people. I met Harlotte, her roommate Emma and then spent a good deal of time with Jimmy McNaughton, just going over things."

"What do you think?"

"I think Harlotte's lucky if she gets five minutes alone in the bathroom. They have someone with her virtually all the time. Jimmy's even got someone posted outside her hotel room twenty-four seven. After your bout tomorrow night, they're back on the bus and heading to Chicago. I don't think there's enough time for anything to happen."

"God, I hope not, no one would be happier than me if there wasn't an incident."

"So, you think you might skate better tomorrow if I came over tonight, maybe gave you a full body massage?"

"No."

"You want to think about it a little bit before you jump to any hasty conclusions?"

"No. The last thing I need is to show up at work on about three hours of sleep, work all day and then skate. Thanks, but no thanks.

"Really?"

"Yeah, really. I might be ready for some assistance in a victory celebration after tomorrow night's bout."

"I could do that, but what happens if you don't win?"

"You just better hope that we do."

"Okay, well, enjoy your evening. I'm going to be with the Hustlers at breakfast tomorrow morning. I'll see you tomorrow night."

"Thanks, Dev."

"Goodnight, Spankie."

Eight

Breakfast with the Hastings Hustlers consisted of a feeding frenzy billed as a buffet. Platters of bacon and eggs, side dishes of French toast, and pancakes treading in pools of maple syrup topped off by caramel rolls and muffins, all inhaled by the ladies and then washed down by about fifty pots of tea.

"How'd you sleep?" I asked.

Jimmy nodded.

Emma moved her neck around like she was warming up for a boxing match.

"Just fine," Harlotte said.

"The girls have a light warm-up this morning. We'll leave here about half-ten," Jimmy said.

"Is that nine-thirty?" I asked.

"No, I think you'd say half-past-ten. We're back here for lunch at half-one. They take it easy, rest up for tonight's event, and we're back on the bus to Chicago immediately after that."

"What time will you be going back to the arena?"

"Tonight?"

"Yeah"

Emma excused herself and headed back to the buffet trays.

"Just after six," Jimmy said. "I'm wondering if you wouldn't mind staying there, at the arena, keeping an eye on the locker room. Staff over there said they would, but my experience is they'll be running around attending to last minute bits and bobs and won't be bothered."

"Yeah, probably a good idea." I was thinking it might make even more sense if I was in the locker room while the Hustlers showered and changed.

"We can post you outside the door once the team arrives," Jimmy said, shattering my dream.

Emma returned with a plate of pancakes buried under about two pounds of bacon.

"You've spoken with your police?" Fiona asked.

"I spoke with them yesterday. I plan to contact them again today while you're practicing, just to touch base. I've a point of contact in the homicide division," I said, trying to impress.

"Who's that? What's the chap's name, just in case?" Jimmy said. He'd pulled a pen out of thin air and sat ready to write in a small notebook.

"Detective Norris Manning." I gave Manning's phone number to Jimmy, pretty sure a phone conversation with Manning would do nothing to improve international relations.

"Hopefully, I won't have to talk with him," Jimmy said.

"Hopefully."

At a quarter to eleven, I was following the Hustlers bus on I-94 into downtown St. Paul. I kept glancing in the rearview mirror, checking for anyone who might be following. If anyone was, they were too good for me to spot. I spent the entire practice session sitting inside the Hustlers locker room. Exciting as that may sound, it wasn't.

I placed a call to Manning in homicide, just to touch base. I waited the requisite ten minutes before a voice came back on the line.

"He's ahhh, busy right now, Mr. Haskell. Is there anything I could help you with?"

"No, not really, if I could just leave the message I phoned. I'm with the Hastings Hustlers. I just wanted to check in."

"I'll be sure to let him know you're with the Hastings Hustlers."

"Thanks, I'd appreciate that," I said, getting the distinct feeling Manning was sitting next to the guy and probably on his third donut.

I toyed with the idea of hiding in the locker room until the Hustlers were all in the shower and then jumping out, but with my luck that karate black belt Emma Babe would be there and break my arm, just for fun. Jimmy opened the door and saved me from myself.

"Okay, Dev, the team's on the way in, so you can stretch your legs outside here. Once they've showered up, we'll get them back on the bus."

The locker room door opened wider, and a couple of the Hustlers began to roll in. I twiddled around for another few minutes, hoping for a cheap shot that never happened, and then Jimmy led both of us out.

"I know, what you're thinking," he said, as we leaned against the wall outside the locker room. "After a while, I don't even notice they're naked. I've seen so much of it."

"They weren't," I said, disappointed.

The remainder of the afternoon proved to be just as exciting. The Hustlers returned to the hotel, had lunch, and then adjourned to their rooms to watch soap operas or whatever they did. I busied myself sitting in the locker room back at the auditorium, reading a brochure about things to do while in St. Paul. Half the things to do turned out to be in Minneapolis. I did make note of the fact that assault by frenzied twenty-something dancers jumping around at the Dew Drop was not listed.

A little after six, the team was loaded on the bus with their luggage and driven back into downtown St. Paul. I was napping on a bench when they arrived.

Nine

ven downstairs in the bowels of the auditorium, standing outside the locker room, you could hear the crowd overhead. Not a roar, but a constant hum. I was waiting with Jimmy in the hallway. He'd escort the team out to the track and remain with them out there. I'd post myself in the locker room, again, until they returned at halftime.

"So far, so good." Jimmy winked.

"That's why I make all the big bucks. This excitement," I said.

"Anytime now, gentlemen," some official called down the hall in our direction.

Jimmy nodded and knocked on the locker room door. A moment later, the Hustlers began to roll out. On wheels, a number of them were my height or taller. I nodded at anyone who made eye contact. During practice earlier in the day, they wore sweat pants and grungy sweatshirts. This was a far cry.

They had black, and pink striped stockings pulled up to the knees over fishnet hose. The uniform was black, a sleeveless one piece that formed into really tight hot pants. There were pink letters across everyone's ass that read 'Stay-Up.' Emblazoned red and yellow flames shot up their thighs. Their names, printed in pink, Gothic style script, ran across their shoulders.

Harlotte Davidson was in the lead. Her makeup was a bit on the severe side, eyebrows penciled to an arch, rouged cheeks, hot pink eye shadow that drew to a point somewhere off to the side of her face. Ruby red lips outlined with a darker red. Not what I usually liked, but sexy in a different way.

"Good luck," I said.

"Thanks." She shrugged and smiled back.

Emma was close behind her, rolling her shoulders back and forth.

"Good luck, Emma," I said.

She grunted back, but never looked at me.

"All right," Jimmy called. "Just like always follow me, stay close. Okay, let's go."

They rolled out of the hallway, and I could hear the growing roar of the crowd as they skated into the auditorium. I waited for a minute or two, then knocked on the locker room door. When I didn't hear anything, I opened the door and called into the room.

"Anyone in here?"

All I heard was the crowd overhead and the unintelligible voice of an announcer. I walked into the locker room and sat on one of the benches. I looked around at the individual locker areas. It was and wasn't like other locker rooms I'd been in. The sinks and showers were at the far end, white hexagonal tile on the floor with glazed brick walls. I thought I could hear some water dripping. All that seemed to fit.

I heard the national anthem playing overhead.

Maybe it was the various frilly lace items hanging from hooks, or the fact that the room smelled reasonably nice. Maybe it was the thousand dollars worth of hair care products on the upper shelf of each locker area. I don't know. There didn't seem to be that sense of abandoned litter and trash so common in men's locker rooms. I wasn't sure any of the girls in here would ever get snapped with a wet towel or have their clothes stolen while they were taking a shower.

I heard the crowd roar overhead and more muffled announcer commentary. The bout must have started. There was a big part of me that wanted to watch Spankie and the Bombshells take on Harlotte Davidson and the Hastings Hustlers. Instead, I was down here, guarding a locker room full of woman's underwear.

I thought about stealing all their towels, maybe adjusting the showers, so they just sprayed cold water. Then thought maybe it would be a better idea if I didn't play the clown for once and just made sure they got out of town without an incident.

Overhead the crowd roared.

Ten

I may have dozed off again, but I couldn't be sure. Either way, I jerked my head up just as the door opened, and a number of red faced, sweaty women rolled into the locker room.

"Bloody hell," someone screamed and flung a helmet across the room.

"We're getting our bleeding arses handed to us," another shouted.

I figured it was probably inappropriate to ask how things were going. The place suddenly took on that familiar locker room smell.

"I'll kill that redheaded American bitch," Emma growled, rolling in the door. She shoved one of the girls aside, repeatedly slammed her helmet against the cinderblock wall, then turned and glared at me, the only American in the room.

"Dev," Jimmy called from the door. "Join me out here for a bit."

He didn't have to tell me twice. I headed for the door, giving Emma a wide berth.

She glared at me as I retreated to the safety of the hallway.

"How's it going?" I asked Jimmy once the door closed behind me. I had to talk over the catfight coming from inside the locker room. You could hear the girls swearing and screaming at one another on the far side of the door. It sounded like they were about to kill one another.

"Seems to be going our way at the moment." Jimmy shrugged.

"You kidding? God, I'd hate to be around if they were having a bad day."

"Just letting off some steam."

"Could have fooled me," I said.

"They'll get over it."

I recalled my daydream about hiding in the locker room and jumping out when they were all in the shower. Good thing I didn't pursue that thought, they were liable to do more to me than just cut off a finger.

"Anytime now, gentleman." The same guy called down the hallway a few minutes later.

Jimmy knocked on the locker room door and then called, "It's time, ladies."

After a moment, the girls rolled out, lined up behind Jimmy just like before, only now they were a lot sweatier.

"Good luck, Fiona," I said to Harlotte.

"The crowd really likes me," she said, then smiled and shrugged back.

I nodded at a couple of other girls. Emma stood about four women back. She did not look happy. I decided to give her a dose of my personal charm.

"Good luck, Em…"

"Piss off, Yank." Emma grabbed me by the neck, spit on me, and shoved me against the wall.

I pushed back against her boobs with both hands. It was just a reaction, nothing intentional. She rolled backward into the wall, then charged right back at me and gave a Karate kick. I tried to block the kick by grabbing her leg and pulling it past me, forgetting she was on wheels.

Her eyes widened when her supporting leg rolled out from underneath her, and she shrieked as she went down, bouncing her head off the concrete floor. Fortunately, she was wearing her helmet. As she hit the floor, a loud "Uff" came out of her mouth. She laid there, eyes wide as I stood over her, still holding her ankle.

A number of her teammates screamed. Jimmy turned round to see what the commotion was. Harlotte rolled against the far wall, mouth open and eyes wide.

"Are you mental? What the hell are you doing?" Jimmy screamed.

Clearly, I wasn't thinking.

"For God's sake, let her go, you stupid bastard, let her go," he screamed.

I let go of Emma's ankle, and it dropped to the floor like a lead weight, eliciting another "Uff" when it hit the concrete floor.

One of the ladies hit me over the head with her helmet, someone else kicked me with her roller skate, and
suddenly things went black.

Eleven

We were in the security office of the auditorium. A cinderblock room painted grey and devoid of any windows or personality. There was a handwritten roster taped to the wall, next to last year's calendar.

"So let me get this straight, Miss Felicity Bard, all one-hundred-and-seven-pounds of her and on roller skates, asks you to please not bother her. And you decide it would be funny to fondle her? Squeeze her breasts? Then when she reacts, attempts to fend you off, you turn the thing into a full-blown assault? In front of witnesses. That about right?"

I was sitting on a desk chair with wheels, my hands handcuffed behind me. A fat guy in a grey uniform with a gold badge pinned on his chest sat on the edge of the desk and leaned over me. He was a sergeant named Wayne, according to his name tag, and he had been reading me the riot act. I knew he was a sergeant because his iron-on patch read Security Sergeant.

Detective Norris Manning leaned against the wall behind him, arms folded, eyes sparkling, enjoying the show. He occasionally cracked his gum and never stopped smiling.

"Look, with all due respect, Sergeant," I emphasized the last word. "I don't have to answer you. You're the security guard at a now empty auditorium. You're not the police." I looked past him. "I haven't been read my rights," I called to Manning.

"We'll get to that soon enough, douche bag. Far as I can tell, the sergeant here is just doing his job. He pursued and detained an abusive individual, you. That same individual, you, was involved in an assault on a young woman earlier tonight, one Felicity Bard, AKA Emma Babe."

"Come on, assault? It was self-defense, there were witnesses."

"Oh, yeah, that's right, there were witnesses. Seven, Sergeant? Is that correct?"

"Seventeen," Sergeant Wayne replied. He continued to stare down at me, then rubbed his right fist into the palm of his left hand and glared some more.

"And they were all witnesses? To an assault?"

"You got it. They all signed statements saying this jerk attacked that little English girl down in the hallway outside the visiting women's locker room."

"Lurking outside a woman's locker room sounds predatory." Manning smiled.

"I want my lawyer," I said.

"Lawyer? You're not even in our custody, yet." Manning grinned. "You know, Sergeant, there's been a bit of a history with someone stalking these English girls, ever since they arrived in the US."

"Really?" Sergeant Wayne sat up. I could tell because his rolls of fat rearranged themselves, and stretched the buttons of his shirt to the breaking point. He never took his eyes off me.

"Yeah, it seems someone has been mailing them body parts, following them around."

"Body parts?"

"Yeah, to those little English girls, can you imagine? What kind of limp wristed bastard would do that?" Manning said and then smiled at me, eyes twinkling.

Wayne nodded, and glared down at me, thinking he knew exactly the kind of bastard. I could sense the wheels inside his thick skull slowly begin to turn.

"Knock this shit off, Manning. You're going to get Sergeant Schultz here all excited. They were fingers Wayne, fingers."

Wayne's eyes grew large and he turned to Manning.

"There's your confession, Detective. This bastard just admitted it, and it didn't take me too long.

"Manning, knock this shit off and get me out of here. You know I didn't have anything to do with that shit. We talked about it on the phone yesterday."

"See, Wayne, it's not uncommon for your serial killers, stalkers and the like to crave publicity. They're always trying to prove they're smarter than folks like you and me. They're always trying to prove themselves smarter than those of us actually involved in day-to-day law enforcement."

"Get me the hell out of here. Come on, Manning," I pleaded.

"Okay, since he's confessed, I guess we'll take it from here," Manning said after a long moment.

Wayne nodded then yanked my arms up behind my back to unlock his handcuffs.

"Ouch, Jesus, will you watch it. What the hell's wrong with you, Wayne?"

He pulled me close, hissing at me. From his breath, I guessed he'd spent a good part of the night protecting the Bratwurst stand.

"I better not see your worthless ass in my auditorium, ever again."

"Your auditorium? God, get me out of here, Manning. Come on."

Twelve

ouie Laufen, my attorney, was slurring his words. Even over the noise from the jukebox in whatever bar he was in, I could hear that much.

"Look, Dev, trust me on this. As your personal legal advisor, I'm telling you it would be a really bad idea for me to get my fat ass down there tonight. I've had a couple of drinks."

"Louie, can you call someone else to come down and get me out of here tonight? I don't want to spend the night locked up in a jail cell."

"No, no, what's the score?" I guessed he was talking to whoever was seated next to him at the bar.

"Louie!"

"Hello, who's this?"

It ended up being almost noon the following day before I was released.

"Look Dev, what are you pissed off at me for? I came as soon as you called," Louie said. We were standing on the sidewalk outside of the Ramsey County Jail. Cars were backed up along Kellogg Boulevard in both directions due to the road construction.

"You came as soon as I called? Louie, I called you last night."

"You did? When?"

"After they brought me in, as soon as I could get to a phone."

"No shit. Well, why didn't you leave a message?"

"A message? I talked with you, man, but you said you couldn't come down."

"Mmm-mmm, actually, that was probably a pretty good idea, me not coming down. No, I don't think I would have helped last night. Well, no real harm done," he said and slapped me on the shoulder.

"No real— I spent the night in jail, Louie."

"Not the first time, Dev. Can I drop you some-where?"

"Yeah, as a matter of fact, if it hasn't been towed, I have to pick up my car at the Veteran's Auditorium."

"That's not exactly on my way, I was—"

"No real harm done," I said, then slapped him on the shoulder and glared.

"Okay, okay, come on, I'll give you a lift."

My car hadn't been towed, but only because they hadn't gotten to it yet. It was ticketed for a tow, parked in an overnight spot that you weren't supposed to park in overnight.

"Damn it, a hundred-and-twenty-five bucks," I said, tossing the ticket into my front seat.

"Count your blessings. It would have been two-twenty-five if they towed you over to the impound lot," Louie said, then waved and drove off. Mr. Positive.

I drove home to shower, change, and use a bathroom where I could close the door. I was getting undressed and pulled my phone out of my pocket to set it on the dresser. I had four messages and a-half-dozen texts. All had come through while I had been in custody. The first text was from Jimmy short and to the point, *'U'r fired.'* The next five were from Justine, but I didn't have the heart to read them. I deleted them all and moved onto the voice mail. They were all from Justine, too. I was about to learn she could be a woman of few words.

"Dev, you okay?"

"Dev, call me."

"Are you crazy?"

"Don't call me."

I called her and had to leave a message.

"Hi Justine, its Dev. There seems to be a slight misunderstanding about last night. I'd like to explain. Please call. Thank you."

I took a long, hot shower. I hosed off the woman's locker room, the assault, my interrogation, a night in the cell next to the drunk tank, and the fifteen-minute ride in Louie's car. In the shower, I discovered a knot on the top of my head where one of those reactionary English chicks had clubbed me with her helmet.

Justine didn't return my call. I got dressed and drove to the office. I stuffed two quarters in the slot, and grabbed a copy of the morning paper from the box on the corner. I climbed the stairs, and made some coffee up in my office. I poured what amounted to barely half a cup then opened up the paper. There, in the bottom corner of the front page, **Local Man Assaults English Girl**, story page 3. Wonderful.

The article, written by a James Tarbox, was three paragraphs long. I couldn't recall talking with this hack. It was accompanied by a stock photo of Felicity Bard, AKA Emma Babe. In the photo she was bending down, resting her hands on the shoulders of three cherub-like children at a London Heart Hospital. In the photo, Emma looked like an innocent fourteen-year-old with big boobs. The article gave all the pertinent details, she weighed one-hundred-and-seven pounds, stood five-feet-two-inches, and was over here fundraising at her own expense so the hospital could purchase a CT scanner for children. She'd been hospitalized overnight for observation. Mercifully my name wasn't mentioned. I was simply described as "a local man known to police."

My phone rang, dragging me out of the daydream where I was shoving Emma in her roller skates off a ramp and into the Grand Canyon.

"Hello?"

"I'm returning your call."

"Justine, thanks for calling." I waited a very long moment for a response, but there wasn't one. "Hello?"

"I'm returning your call."

"Thank you. Look, I just wanted to explain. I didn't mean for things to get out of hand last night. God, it seems like everyone has just jumped to a conclusion and…"

"Jumped to a conclusion? For your information, there are about a million witnesses. We were all hauled in to talk to the head of security at the Veteran's Auditorium…"

"That lard ass Wayne guy?"

"I don't know his name, but he's the sergeant in charge. To tell you the truth, we were all just a little too shocked to get his name."

"He's not some sergeant. That's just the name of the security company that—"

"I don't think any of that is really important right now. We're looking at a potential lawsuit here. I've spent the better part of last night and all of this morning doing damage control with the media."

"A lawsuit?"

"We were stupid enough to hire you and put you in touch with the Hastings Hustlers. You said it wouldn't be a problem. Now you've moved us to the top of the list, thanks a bunch. By the way, you failed to mention it would be the shit list. I've been talking to lawyers all morning." She was yelling at this point.

"Tell me about it."

"I, in fact, we, have been advised not to have any contact with you. So that's the only reason I'm calling, I wanted to tell you personally that I'm not talking to you."

"Well, at least they're in Chicago, so you can get back—"

"Oh, haven't you heard? They're still here, the Hustlers. Chicago cancelled. Seems what with the finger thing and now the assault from a local nut case up here, Chicago just doesn't need the hassle. So they canceled. I'm sure the remaining cities on the tour will follow suit before the day is over. Nice job, Dev, we've worked years to build up the image, do all sorts of good, and you managed to destroy everything in about fifteen seconds."

"Hey, that woman assaulted me. I'm the victim here. I— Hello. Hello? Justine?"

There was probably nothing positive to be gained by calling back and suggesting we'd been cut off.

Thirteen

I figured if I phoned Jimmy McNaughton, he'd either refuse to see me or contact Justine and then refuse to see me, so instead, I drove over to the Hustlers hotel. Jimmy was in the dining room drinking tea. He was English, after all. From what I could tell, the Hustlers were grazing on double cheeseburgers, double orders of fries, and washing it all down with diet cokes.

"What the hell do you think you're doing here? I'm about to call your police," he said the moment he saw me.

"Jimmy, I want to explain. I didn't do anything last night. I was just protecting myself. I'm sorry things developed the way they did. It wasn't my intention—"

"Developed the way they did? You make it sound like you spilled a glass of wine on the carpet. Our tour is about to fall apart, the team enforcer has a sprained shoulder and a bone chip in her heel, and you don't like the way things developed? Bloody hell!" He was red-faced, heading toward purple.

"I was just trying to block her kick."

"You stupid little wanker, she kicked you because you grabbed her boobs," he hissed, then looked around to see if he had attracted any attention.

"I didn't grab her boobs. She spit on me, grabbed me by the throat, told me to piss off, and pushed me against the wall. It was just my natural reaction to push back. That's all I did. The next thing I know, she came flying back with a Karate kick. I just blocked her, and down she went. If she hadn't tried to kick me, how in the hell do you think I got hold of her ankle?"

He seemed to think about that for a moment.

"She said piss off?"

"Yeah, as a matter of fact, she said, 'Piss off, Yank.' Not a reason to assault anyone, I agree, but put it all together, it's just what happened. I'm the one who was attacked here, not her. Then they clubbed me over the head, knocked me out," I said, looking around the room. All the girls suddenly seemed to be making themselves scarce.

"I'm not going to press charges or anything. I'm sorry if she's injured, I just wanted to apologize and set the record straight. That's all."

"Piss off, Yank," he said absently. "Hmm-mmm, yeah, sounds a bit like her."

My relief must have been obvious. Jimmy seemed to be deep in thought.

"Is there some way I can still help you?" I asked.

"Well, I think for the time being, we better have you stay away from the team. They might want to cut off more than your finger."

Not the first time the thought had crossed my mind. Staying away sounded like a good plan to me.

"Have you had any other incidents, any notes, phone calls, any more fingers?"

"No, as of last night, most of our time has been taken up with the likes of you."

"Let me see what I can find out on the finger front, all right?" I said.

Jimmy seemed to consider this for a moment and then nodded. "Just as long as you stay away from the team. They've enough on their plate right now with the tour going all to hell."

"You got it. Thanks, Jimmy," I said and held out my hand.

He took it, shaking with a firm grip.

"Now, please, let me finish my tea in peace."

Fourteen

The logical place to start seemed to be The Spot bar. I strolled in for a late liquid lunch of Leinenkugel beer.

"Dev, you fall down on the job last night?" Jimmy asked as he poured my tap beer.

"Huh?"

"Didn't you tell us you were going to be hanging around that bunch of English girls, providing security? I read in the paper one of them was attacked by some nut case last night. Cute little thing had her picture in the paper with some kids. You see it?"

"The paper? No, haven't had the chance yet. I wasn't at the auditorium last night."

"How'd you know it happened there if you didn't see the paper?" He pushed my beer in front of me, waiting for my reply.

"Heard a couple of them talking about it when they got back to the hotel. That's where I was all night. Just came from there, as a matter of fact, planning strategy."

"Strategy?" He seemed to consider this but didn't add anything else.

After the liquid lunch, I went back to the office and started making phone calls. Over the course of the afternoon, I spoke with the police in Denver, Chicago, St. Louis, and Kansas City. I decided it might be best to work backward, so I called Denver first and ended up speaking with a Detective named Kingston Quinn, who sounded decidedly more black than Irish.

"Detective Quinn, thanks for taking my call. I'm working with Detective Norris Manning up here. We're looking into an incident involving an English roller derby team, the Hastings Hustlers. They—"

"Bunch of fine looking ladies, you ask me. You get to talk with any of 'em?"

"Yes, as a matter of fact, I spoke with some of them as recently as last night. We're interested—"

"Bunch of little hotties and when they talk, I'd like to take all of 'em home, except the wife wouldn't be too happy with that."

"Yeah, who could blame her. Anyway, last night—"

"Yeah, saw something about that come across here. You're up there in St. Paul, right?"

"That's correct. See I wanted to ask a couple of questions regarding the envelope—"

"Yeah, some head case up there attacked one of those hot little girls? Listen, you need any help, couple of us be on the next plane, get that action solved real quick. Then maybe spend a little time with the girls. You know, just to—"

"That's very considerate of you, Detective, but I think the media may have blown that story out of proportion. See the individual they—"

"Little girl barely a hundred pounds gets herself attacked by some jackass, like to cut more than a finger off of that dude, if you catch my drift. See how tough he is after I get through with him."

"We'll keep it in mind. Now about that envelope taped to the door of the bus."

Once we established he was available to spend time with a room full of sexy English girls, Kingston Quinn didn't have a lot more to offer.

"Waiting on the analysis reports to come back. Not sure if you got budget cuts happening up there, but we're dealing with that problem in every department, not to mention one or two more serious issues, you catch my drift."

"I do, unfortunately. Any guess when you might see a report? We talking another week, two?"

"No, more like four to six months."

"Four to sixth months?" I half-shouted.

"No one's called in to say they're missing a finger. We can do some cross-referencing, but it would only be for the greater Denver area. We aren't hooked into other departments around the state, let alone the rest of the country."

"Anyone call the Feds?"

"The FBI? On a finger? That's what we need, a bunch of suits coming in here and screwing up the three thousand plus on-going investigations so we can see who taped a finger to the door of a bus. Not sure how you guys work up there, but we like to stay as far away as possible from those folks."

"Any guesses?"

"You mean, who taped the damn thing to the door?"

"Yeah?"

"Some jackass, just like the jackass who attacked that little girl up there last night. My guess, check him out. He certainly sounded stupid enough."

"Thanks, we're doing that," I said.

"Look, I get a chance I'll make a call, see if they got anything, but with the budget cuts and all, who knows."

"Anything you can do would be appreciated."

Things didn't seem to go a whole lot better in Chicago. I spoke to a Sergeant Anthony Howe with a decided south side Chicago accent.

"St. Paul…huh, something about that sitting on my desk when I came in this morning. You guys nail that flake been sending fingers to them English broads?"

"We're working on it. That's what I wanted to talk to you about."

"You ask me, it's that piece of shit attacked one of those girls up there last night. Let me question the son-of-a-bitch for about five minutes, I'll get you answers, the answers ya want. Still got the bastard locked up? Or did he get all lawyered up and he's out on the street? Probably casing some grade school as we speak. I tell you the court system in—"

"Sergeant Howe, did you process that finger, the one that was sent to the Hastings Hustlers?"

"Yeah, in a manner of speaking."

"Manner of speaking?"

"I don't know how things are up there. Maybe you don't have a lot of scum bags like we do. With all the bad apples we got down here, some guy mails a finger, folks down here probably just worried he got the right postage on the envelope. You know? What the hell, you guys dealing with an occasional assault with an icicle or something, right?" He laughed at his own joke.

"You said you had the finger processed?"

"The one that got mailed?"

"Yeah, with the correct postage."

"Huh? Yeah, we sent it in, ain't come back yet. Like I said, matter of priorities. With the budget cuts and all—"

When I could get a word in edgewise, I thanked him for his time. I got the same response in Kansas City. It wasn't a priority and with budget cuts.

The guy in St. Louis spoke with a lisp, a Detective Sexton. He had the same story as the others, no results, he'd call me when the reports came back, but don't wait by the phone. "Look, I'll give you a call when they come in, but you're probably looking at months, not weeks. Budget cuts and all that shit."

"Yeah, that's what everyone seems to be fighting," I said, it sounded like a broken record.

"God, it's getting worse than dealing with the bad guys. So you work with some guy named Manning up there?"

"Yeah," I said, immediately getting cautious, sensing I was being pushed out onto thin ice.

"That guy as big a jerk as he sounds like on the phone?"

"No, bigger."

"Figures, some things never change. Look, got a few hundred irons in the fire just a little hotter than this. I run into anything, I'll let you know. Okay?"

"Appreciate your time."

An afternoon wasted.

Fifteen

I was sitting in The Spot when my phone rang. I had stopped in to check for messages and nurse a Leinenkugel before I went home.

"Haskell Investigations."

I had to step out the side door to hear as I answered my cell. The jukebox was blaring Bob Seger singing about Old Time Rock and Roll.

"Detective Dev Haskell?"

"You got him."

"King Quinn, Denver. We spoke earlier. This your office phone?"

"No, my cell, I'm out at a crime scene right now."

"Crime scene?" he said, not sounding too convinced.

"Did you find anything for me?"

"No, meaning yes. Nothing turned up in a DNA match. Either someone's not in the CODIS database or, well, that's just it. They're not in the database."

"Meaning?"

"Meaning whoever is missing that finger, they most likely aren't or weren't a sex offender or convicted of a violent felony in the past umpteen years."

"Back to square one."

"Yeah, I can tell you this much. That finger was from a Caucasian male. Aged between twenty-five and forty, and one other thing."

"What's that?"

"It was frozen, the finger."

"Frozen?"

"Yeah, not when we recovered it, but it had been frozen."

"What sense does that make? Why?"

"Maybe this guy has a stash of them, on ice. When he needs one, he grabs it out of the freezer and mails it off."

"Or tapes it to the door of a bus," I added.

"That too," he said.

"Of course, which suggests someone who has access to them, the fingers."

"Maybe a hospital worker, morgue, undertaker, someone along those lines," he said, thinking out loud.

"Yeah, maybe. Detective, thanks for the effort and the call back. You come across anything else, please let me know."

"Sure thing, Detective," he said the last word like he wasn't quite sure, but played the party line just in case. Then followed up with, "Give my best to all those English girls."

"I will."

"And Detective Manning."

"I'll be sure to let him know."

"Just kidding. Don't," he said and hung up.

Actually, the smart thing to do would be to call Manning in homicide, give him the information I'd just received and let him follow it up. Instead, I called the guy in St. Louis with a lisp, Sexton. He didn't speak too kindly about Manning, and I hoped to maybe use that to my advantage. I left a message.

Next, I phoned Jimmy McNaughton, just to touch base. I treaded carefully after all he might have been in touch with Manning.

"What can I do for you?" Jimmy asked, sounding preoccupied.

"Just keeping you up to date. So far, none of those fingers match up to anyone in our databases here."

"Your contact with the police tell you this?"

"Manning? No, actually, he's got a lot on his plate right now. I went ahead and contacted the other departments, Denver, St. Louis, Chicago, and Kansas City. I wanted to see what I could learn from them."

"And what'd you learn?"

"Just what I said, they can't get a match to anyone here in the states. I thought if we could find where the fingers came from, it would help in finding out who sent them." I purposely didn't tell Jimmy about the finger in Denver having been frozen.

"Felicity was released this noon from your Regions Hospital," Jimmy said.

"Oh, I hope she's okay."

"Probably best for both of us not to comment at this stage. I did get a visit from three of the girls."

"A visit?"

"Seems they wanted to withdraw their statements."

"The statements about what happened between Emma and me, that bullshit about groping and attacking her? Fantastic, they came to their senses and said nothing like that happened. That it?"

"Not exactly. They said they were too far away and maybe just joined up in the heat of the moment. Thought better of it and as much as they'd like to see you brought to justice, upon further reflection, they didn't see enough to sign a statement."

"It's a start and I'll take it. Listen, Jimmy, I'm going to check back with the other departments I spoke with today. I hear anything else, I'll let you know."

"Thanks, I'd appreciate that."

I wandered back inside The Spot, finished my beer, and went home.

Sixteen

I was on my laptop, supposedly doing a search on frozen fingers and anything that might point to a copycat situation. In actuality, I was drinking beer and watching a porn video titled No Boys Allowed, hoping to learn something about women's sports teams. Thus far, I'd learned a lot, none of which could be applied to women sports teams in general or the Hastings Hustlers specifically. The cellphone broke my concentration.

"Haskell Investigations."

"Hello, Dev, this is Justine."

I deleted the sound to hide the nonstop moaning and tore myself away from the computer screen.

"I'm sorry, am I interrupting something?"

"Justine, hi, hello, thanks for calling. Everything okay?"

"Yeah, as a matter of fact, a lot better than yesterday. I just got off the line with our manager. She got a call from the Hustlers and Emma Babe. Her name's actually Felicity Bard. Anyway, she's been released from the hospital."

This wasn't news to me.

"Well good, I hope she's doing well," I said, trying to sound sincere all the while visualizing me tripping the little bitch and pushing her down the hundred steps in front of the Saint Paul Cathedral.

"Oh, yeah, I guess she'll be fine. But, the reason I called is some of the girls over there have changed their story."

"Changed their story?"

"Yeah, you know, swearing to things they said they saw you do."

"Things they saw me do, like assault Emma Babe and grab her by her boobs?"

"Well, yeah."

"I'm glad to hear that. Any help I can get in not becoming public enemy number one is always appreciated."

"I guess fourteen of the girls have said they really didn't see anything."

"Fourteen, that's great. Didn't see anything? You mean they weren't watching or that it didn't happen the way your pal Emma said it did?"

"They said they were too far away, but at least they've withdrawn their statements. That's the important thing. And, just for the record, she's not my pal."

"There were seventeen signed statements, so just Emma and two others still have statements out there. Right?" I said.

"Yeah, I'm guessing she'll stick to what she said, but it's encouraging," Justine actually sounded upbeat.

"It's very encouraging. Now, if we could just get things back on track and find out who is stalking Harlotte Davidson."

There was a long pause.

"Look, Dev, sorry if maybe I may have jumped to a little conclusion. You know, about you grabbing Emma and all."

Gee, sexual assault, stalking, predatory behavior, battery. Nice little conclusion, I thought.

"I understand, Justine. I think under the circumstances, I may have done the same. The good news is it's working out, and people are coming to their senses."

Another long pause.

"Well, I just wanted to be the one to let you know. Hopefully, we can dodge the legal bullet."

"That would be nice."

I thought about asking her over for a half dozen beers, maybe try out my shower in the morning, but decided it might not be the best move right now. Besides, I'd already downloaded No Boys Allowed.

Seventeen

I heard back from the cops in St. Louis and Kansas City the following afternoon. I told them about the frozen finger and no DNA match out of Denver. Neither one seemed particularly interested. Amazing they had bigger fish to fry than worrying about what some idiot did to a traveling team who had already come and gone.

I searched online for anything remotely looking like a copycat incident and found absolutely nothing. Justine phoned me late in the afternoon.

I was staring out my office window, watching women get off the bus across the street. Thirty-something's, city or state workers, I guessed, finished at four every day and able to bus to and from work. Perhaps wisely, not a one of them ventured into The Spot. My cellphone pulled me back to reality.

"Haskell Investigations."

"Hi Dev, Justine."

"Justine, what's up?"

"Just got a call from our manager, the last two girls have withdrawn their statements, so it's just Emma holding out."

"She'll stick to her story, but she's standing all alone if it ever goes to court. My guess is it's not going anywhere at this stage. If they went to all the trouble of withdrawing their statements, they aren't going to switch back again in a courtroom. I'm guessing they won't charge me."

"That's a relief," she said, then waited.

"What's next?"

"They're still trying to put together some semblance of a schedule. We might be having a bout in the next few nights just to help them out. I don't know, seems like everything just pretty much up and fizzled."

"Well, no offense, but I think I'll watch the next bout from the stands. Keep me posted when it's happening."

"Yeah, I'll do that. Well, I better run." She waited a moment, giving me time to say something. "See ya," she finally said and hung up.

I wasn't ready to ask Justine over, and I wasn't sure I ever would be. I looked absently out the window and debated about getting an early start over at The Spot when my cellphone rang. No doubt, Justine calling with some sweet offer.

"Haskell Investigations," I said, sounding busy, too busy.

"Hey, have you even started looking through those applications I sent you?"

"Andy?"

"Yes, Andy. Who else gave you a stack of job applications to verify? Don't tell me you're screwing up two companies, the other one owned by some poor guy with the same name as me."

"Actually, I've got them finished. I can get them over to you tonight if you like."

"I like. We can't get anything done over here until we have them. The phone has been ringing off the hook with well-intentioned, desperate folks calling to see if they're getting a second interview."

"I'll have them to you in an hour."

"That would be nice. Any surprises?"

"Actually, no, nothing out of the ordinary. A couple of dates maybe extended, but I'd put them down as honest mistakes. No one listed themselves as CEO when in fact, they were the receptionist if that's what you mean."

"See you in an hour," Andy said and hung up.

Eighteen

It didn't sound like much fun. Andy was the third generation to run what was still a family business. C. Lindbergh Memorials had been founded by Andy's great grandfather, Carlyle, a stonemason. Carlyle Lindbergh had the good fortune to start his business in 1926. One year before Charles Lindbergh, 'Lucky Lindy' (no relation), set off on his epic flight across the Atlantic. In 1928 Carlyle cleverly added the logo of a plane rising up into the clouds.

C. Lindbergh Memorials started out carving tombstones. Andy's father expanded the line to include wooden coffins. Andy took the operation big time, handling everything from toe tags and body bags to embalming supplies and mortuary makeup.

I was standing at the receptionist counter when Andy saw me from his office.

"Send that idiot in here," he yelled.

"He'll see you now, sir," the receptionist said. She was a middle-aged woman with hair the color of something not found in nature. It was just after five, and she stuffed two Tupperware containers into a gigantic purse, then shut down her computer and waved goodbye.

"Any surprises?" Andy said, watching me pull three stacks of applications from a briefcase and place them on his desk.

"No, like I said on the phone, very straightforward. I've noted any discrepancy with a Post-It-Note, but it was all very minor stuff."

"Sounds like it was pretty easy on your end."

"I still had to make the calls. Still had to call back when someone was busy. You've got over three hundred applications, three hundred and seven, to be exact."

"Sign of the times. God, I'd like to hire dozens. They all interviewed well, but it'll only be one or two," he said, shaking his head. He looked at his watch. "It's after five, want a bump?"

"Maybe just one."

Andy's expansive office was what I guessed any CEO's would be like. Well, if you discounted the huge painting of tombstones over the couch against the far wall and the oak panels sporting various coffin handles arrayed along the window sill. I always thought it would be funny if Andy's phone played Taps or Amazing Grace, but kept that suggestion to myself. His desk was covered with files, reports, and pictures of his family. I settled into the comfortable leather chair opposite his desk and waited.

He reached around to a wood box sitting on the credenza that looked like a miniature coffin. The thing was polished burled wood, inlaid with mother of pearl and fancy veneer designs, a gorgeous little bit of craftsmanship. There was a brass plaque on the top of the box with Andy's name exquisitely engraved. He opened the hinged top, the inside was lined with burled wood. He pulled out a bottle of Jameson, then two cut crystal glasses.

"Gee, and to think I knew you when you used to drink beer right out of the tap."

"Nice, isn't it? It's one of our better sellers, gorgeous little thing."

"You're selling liquor cabinets now?"

"No, you kidding? It's an urn."

"An urn?"

"For ashes, you know, after a cremation. Holds a fifth and a couple of glasses rather nicely, don't you think?"

"That's your name on the thing?"

"A little industry humor," he said, pouring.

We chatted on a bit, catching up on various guys one or the other had lost track of overtime. Then I asked, "You follow the news about someone stalking that English roller derby Team?"

Andy took a sip, looking thoughtful for half a moment.

"Just that I think they finally got the guy, didn't they? Some idiot attacked them down at the Veteran's Auditorium. Guess he'd followed them all across the country or something. What an absolute whack job. Where do they come from?"

"Well, that's not exactly right. I think the incident you're referring to was more of a misunderstanding, some poor innocent actually harangued by one of the roller derby women. I don't think that particular situation was the stalker as much as it was one of the women flipping out and going off the deep end."

"Going off the deep end? The story I read said some nut case started grabbing and groping those women, and they eventually beat the shit out of him. Not enough if you ask me. Someone did that to one of my daughters I'd have him lined up to sample a number of our products." He followed up with a healthy sip, then reached around for the bottle. "Hey wait a minute, you weren't involved in that, were you?" He eyed me suspiciously, holding the bottle, ready to pour into my glass, waiting for the correct answer before he commenced.

"No, I wasn't involved," I lied. "I've been working with them, the English team, trying to get a handle on what sort of individual would be doing this."

"That's easy. Like I said, some whack job."

"Yeah, of course. But, part of the stalking has been someone mailing severed fingers to one of the girls."

"Fingers?"

"Yeah, always the middle finger, minus the fingertip, by-the-way. Mailed the things to a couple of different cities where they were. Then in Chicago, he slipped one under the door of the hotel room."

"No shit?"

"So far, none of the fingers correspond to any DNA in the database. Well, actually, we've only been able to get results back on one. By the way, it had been frozen. I mean frozen at some point, not after the thing was delivered."

Andy nodded like this made sense, then took a sip.

"God and people kid me about my business," he said, gazing at the ceiling.

"Andy, how hard would it be for someone in your line of work to acquire fingers?"

"Harder than you think," he said, not blinking. "You're dealing with families. Nowadays, it wouldn't be uncommon to have an open casket prior to the actual funeral service, whether at a mortuary or a church. From there, you're on your way to the cemetery for the graveside service, the casket's locked, lowered, covered then and there. It's pretty traditional for hands to be exposed while the deceased lies in repose. There's family hovering around at all times. It would be very risky for someone to try what you're suggesting, not to mention absolutely crazy on about a dozen different levels."

"What about a morgue?"

"Same process. Think of the morgue as more like a holding facility, but the body is almost always turned over to a mortuary at some point."

"How the hell could someone have access to a steady supply of fingers?" I asked.

"I really can't see it from our industry. Anything's possible, but there are so many checks and balances. So much scrutiny and it's very common for people to be putting a last minute something into the coffin, a letter, a photo. It just would be really difficult. What about some industrial circumstance?"

"Yeah, sure, I can just imagine OSHA going easy on some business where people routinely lose fingers."

"Okay, I get your point."

Andy seemed to think for a long time. Staring at his liquor urn, he sipped some more.

"You know, there is one way, maybe."

"Oh?"

"A crematorium."

"How does that work? The body is reduced to ashes, or in your case a fifth of Jameson," I nodded at the miniature coffin on his desk.

"Actually, it's reduced to dried bits of bone fragments. They grind those up in what's called a cremulator, then—"

"Okay, okay, too much information."

"It's extremely rare that a family would watch the actual cremation. Perhaps, you know, just before that process begins, you could get in there, harvest what you wanted, and any telltale sign would be almost immediately destroyed."

"Harvest?" I asked.

"Yeah, harvest."

Maybe, I thought, then held out my glass for another refill.

"What about a hospital?"

"Sure, it's possible, but for one thing."

"Which is?" I asked, then sipped.

"Hospitals don't amputate healthy fingers. The finger would have to be damaged, severely, before they would amputate. Of course, there are all sorts of procedures and controls for disposal. They don't just toss the things in the dumpster."

That seemed to make sense.

"You said someone had removed the tip of the finger, so the fingerprints couldn't be checked?"

I nodded.

"Well, unless the thing was also severely damaged, which would seem to be obvious to anyone viewing it, I don't think the hospital or a surgery clinic is your source."

"My first thought was something along the lines of a homeless guy or a druggy, but there are four separate incidents of this. You'd think someone, somewhere, would report an attack or something. So I don't know, I guess I'm back to your end of things," I said.

"Possibly," Andy replied and sipped some more Jameson.

Nineteen

The following morning I was in my office, watching co-eds waiting for the bus across the street. They didn't look too happy. Maybe that was just because it was morning and they couldn't stay in bed. Maybe it was exam week. Maybe it was because they were nursing a hangover like mine.

I was thinking about what Andy Lindbergh had told me yesterday, about the difficulty someone at a mortuary would have getting fingers. Harvesting was the term he had used. My cellphone rang, disturbing my complete lack of productivity.

"Haskell Investigations."

"Hi, Dev, it's Justine."

"Hi, Justine, how's it going."

"Pretty good. Say, we got a call from Jimmy McNaughton."

"Yeah," I said, cautious.

"He'd like you to give him a call, would you mind?"

"Any idea what he wants?"

"Yeah, he's going to ask you to talk to Felicity Bard, see if things can't be smoothed out, and everyone can just move on. Would you mind, terribly?"

"She still sticking to her story?"

"I don't know. I would guess yes, she is. But, I understand. I mean, it seems pretty obvious she's lying since all her support has vanished. I think they're just hoping to put the whole thing behind them and move on. We've scheduled a bout with them in a couple of nights. They're trying to resurrect their schedule, get something put together, so the trip over here isn't a complete disaster."

I felt like telling her, yes I minded a lot. Then ask her what my standing was with the Bombshells? Her in particular, but I was still too mad to care. Justine and the Bombshells didn't back me when I needed it, so why should I come to the rescue now? To make my point, I said, "I'd be happy to talk with her, and I'll be happy to call Jimmy."

"Would you mind, terribly?"

Yes, I did mind terribly.

"Not a problem, I'll call him as soon as we're off the line."

"Oh, Dev, that's great. I don't know how to thank you."

I could think of a couple of ways, Spankie, but didn't think it was wise to elaborate just now. I dialed Jimmy's number, and he answered on the second ring. I had a feeling he'd been prepped to expect my call.

"McNaughton."

"Hi, Jimmy, Dev Haskell here. Got a half-minute to chat?"

"I do. How can I help you?"

"Look, I'm wondering if I came over, and had a heart to heart with Felicity if that wouldn't help to smooth things over and maybe we could all get this… ahhh… situation, behind us, and move on."

"I think that's a splendid idea. When can you come over?"

"You name the time and I'll be there."

"We take our lunch at one. They have a team meeting before that. Why don't you plan on arriving oh, say quarter past two? I'll bring you up to their room myself."

"Would you mind staying there, too? No offense, but I don't think it would be the best of ideas to be in there alone with Felicity."

"I can do that. You're probably right."

"See you a little after two, then," I said.

"Best to find me in the dining room. I'll be having my tea."

I thought it would be bad form to bring a baseball bat and beat Felicity across her fat head. So, I arrived dutifully a little after two. As promised, I found Jimmy sipping tea in the hotel dining room.

"Jimmy, nice to see you again."

"Dev, thank you for coming in. Would you care for a tea?"

"No thanks. I'm not really a tea kind of guy."

"Ready to have a go at her highness, then?"

"Yeah, let's do it."

We took the elevator. Nothing was said on the way up to the third floor, nor as we walked down the hall to Felicity and Fiona's room. I noticed the hotel security Jimmy had told me would be permanently stationed outside their room was nowhere in sight.

"You cancel the security you had outside their room?" I asked.

"Combination of things calming down and a bit of the proverbial budget crunch," he said and knocked on the door.

Fiona opened the door almost immediately and gave me the requisite shrug of her shoulders along with a smile.

"Hi, Dev, nice to see you."

"Nice to see you," I said. Jimmy was already walking into the room, and I followed.

"Felicity?" Jimmy asked, looking around.

"Actually, she's not here, Jimmy. I thought she'd be back long before now, but it seems she's not. She wasn't at the team meeting or lunch. You didn't see her downstairs in the dining room?"

"Where the hell did she go?" Jimmy asked.

"Some errand, I don't know. She took a taxi, a bright yellow one," she said to me.

'A bright yellow taxi' didn't really narrow things down. We stood there looking at one another when suddenly the door clicked open, and Felicity, aka Emma Babe, sauntered in. She ignored me, nodded at Jimmy, and walked over to a chair and sat down. She picked up the remote and clicked on the television, then turned in the chair to look out the window at the dumpster and scowled. The television had some muted soap opera.

"Hi, Felicity," I said.

She gave a dismissive nod in my general direction and then went back to staring out the window.

Jimmy smiled and extended a hand, indicating the chair opposite Felicity. I thought about picking up the chair and whacking her over the head with the thing. Not a bad idea. Instead, I asked, "Mind if I sit down?"

"Suit yourself," she said and continued to stare out at the navy blue dumpster in the parking lot.

I gave Jimmy a look, hoped it suggested her flame was waving close to my fuse. If he picked up on my message, he didn't let on. Instead, he smiled and motioned toward the chair with his chin. I sat down, took my time getting comfortable, waiting for her to stop studying the dumpster and look at me, or Jimmy or Fiona. It became apparent that wasn't going to happen.

"Felicity, Jimmy was gracious enough to let me come over and apologize to you about the incident the other night." I swallowed down last night's Jameson rising up from my stomach, gritted my teeth and gripped the arms of the chair.

She continued to stare out the window.

I thought if I hit the back of her head hard enough, her forehead would bounce off the window, and maybe that would get her attention. Oh well, into the Valley of Death.

"I hope you understand it was not my intention to touch you, any part of you, or hurt you in any way. I was simply wishing you good luck, and things maybe got out of—"

"That how you do it over here? Grab me boobs and give the little cow a good squeeze for luck?"

Jimmy and Fiona exchanged glances.

"Well, I think you know I didn't grab you, and anything that happened wasn't intentional on my part."

"Must have been my imagination that had your hands all over me."

"No, it wasn't your imagination. Once you yelled at me to 'piss off', spit on me, and pushed me. I pushed you back to get you away from me, that's all, but—"

"All I know is you landed me in hospital, where they kept me overnight."

Probably looking for a brain, I thought and then felt my fuse igniting.

"Yeah, and believe me, if I had it to do over again, I would have just let you swear at me, spit on me, and kick me, and never reacted. I don't know what I was thinking. So I'm sorry things worked out the way they did. I wish you a speedy recovery and all the best from here on, for you and the entire team," I said, then stood up.

I left out my condolences to everyone who had to deal with this pain-in-the-ass bitch in the future, but I thought my flushed face and the killer glare in my eye got the message across.

Fiona's eyes were wide, while Jimmy sat there red-faced.

"Nice seeing you again. Best of luck in your upcoming bouts. Don't worry, I can show myself out," I said, then opened the door before I picked Emma Bitch up and tossed her out the window.

"I'm really sorry," Fiona whispered, out in the hallway.

"Not a problem, best of luck," I said and continued down the hallway.

"I might still press charges, you wanker," Felicity called from inside the room.

Twenty

I was contemplating humanity, and the terribly complex issues life sometimes presented. I was also drinking a Leinenkugel at The Spot, not my first. It might have been a measure of my mood that I remained on the barstool and answered my cell when it rang, not really caring who was calling or that they might figure out I was in a bar.

"Haskell Investigations."

"Dev? Justine."

I really didn't want to hear that.

"Hi, Justine, how are things?"

"I just wanted to call and say thanks for going over and talking to Felicity this afternoon. It really helped."

"Well, I'm not sure how much it helped, but it's done."

"It's just great to get a bit of a positive spin on things and everything."

"I gotta tell you, Justine, if that was Felicity's idea of a bit of positive spin, it was an extremely tiny bit. I'm not sure much of anything sunk in."

"Yeah, I heard there may have been a little attitude."

"A little attitude? Try talking to a pouty thirteen-year-old on an exceptionally bad day. And that woman does fundraising? I can't imagine she does much."

"That bad, huh?"

"Worse. I don't know what Jimmy or Fiona told you, but let's just say grace does not seem to be Emma's strong suit. Instead of Emma Babe, her name should be Emma Bitch."

"Sorry about that, I really am. We still appreciate your effort going over there and everything. Hopefully, she won't press charges."

"Yeah, well thanks, I appreciate it. I'll live, but you may have an individual on your hands with some real issues, might want to handle with kid gloves. Someone should light a fire under that bitch's ass."

"I'll keep it in mind. Maybe we'll get things settled at our upcoming bout."

"I'd pay to watch. In fact, I'd pay even more to skate against her, maybe just one time around."

"I'll think about that and maybe pass it on. Thanks anyway."

"Appreciate the call, Spankie."

She laughed and hung up.

Against my better judgment, I remained for one more Leinenkugel and then drove home along the back streets. I went online and wasted the next three hours searching for reports of fingers sent to people. I finished up with learning more than I ever needed regarding the cremation business. I never did get around to downloading a porn film.

I spent the next day making collection calls. Not for me, but for a client, City Student Direct. I hated the task, but it paid some bills. I made twenty percent on anything that came in, but making collection calls to people who'd gotten a loan so they could take a couple of classes and maybe get ahead of the game was depressing.

I had the feeling it wasn't working for anyone. A single mom with three intro computer classes did not make a computer programmer. It was depressing for them to get my call and just as depressing for me to make the call.

Fortunately, most of my efforts went unanswered. A few hung up, two cried, and about once an hour, someone agreed to send in a payment. By close to eight that evening, if everyone mailed in what they promised, I'd made about a hundred-and-thirty-seven dollars. Everyone paying what they promised wasn't going to happen, by the way, and I walked across the street to drown my sorrows at The Spot. I ended up closing the place and taking my favorite back route home.

Twenty-one

I woke up a little after the noon hour to a pounding head, at least that was my first thought. It turned out most of the pounding was coming from the patrolmen at my front door, two of them. Another two were stationed at my back door, just in case.

"Devlin Haskell?" The cop asked when I opened the front door. I was in a grungy bathrobe and barefoot. There seemed no point in saying Devlin was upstairs, and they could just go there and get him while I ran down the street.

"Yes, sir, that's me."

"Mr. Haskell, we have a warrant for your arrest . . ." He stood about six foot three, black, maybe two-hundred-and-thirty pounds. The Kevlar vest he wore beneath his blue uniform shirt made him look even more solid, not that he needed it. The name stitched in gold above the flap on his shirt pocket read Tyler, M.

A partner stood off to the side of Officer Tyler, hands resting on his holster belt. His right hand fluttered close to his Taser. He wore a Kevlar vest, too, had almost no neck and biceps that looked to have been blown up to the size of my thighs. He was a white guy with a baby-face. I pegged him for about fourteen years old.

I'd been in this position a couple of times before. I'd been around the block enough times to realize I wasn't going to talk them out of taking me in. It struck me as a wise idea to address both officers as Sir.

"You are Devlin Haskell?"

"Yes, Sir. I'll go with you. Could I take a moment and get dressed?"

They nodded in agreement then followed me inside and upstairs to my bedroom.

"Mr. Haskell, if you could just tell us where your clothes are, we'll retrieve them for you," Tyler said.

I nodded across my bed to the closet and my dresser. I was tempted to tell him to go up into the attic and get the Santa Claus suit I wore to The Spot on Christmas but thought better of the idea.

"I've got jeans right there hanging on the hook. The third drawer down on the dresser is a shirt. Top drawer right is socks, top drawer left is boxers."

Tyler walked around the bed, retrieved the various items, and tossed them my way. I caught a half-smile when he handed me my boxers. A yellow sign that looked like it came from the Highway Department im-printed just above the fly stated 'Open at your own Risk.'

"Cute," Baby Face said, but didn't smile.

Tyler searched the pockets of my jeans before throwing them across the bed. Baby Face still kept a hand close to his Taser. I caught him out of the corner of my eye, glancing up at the mirror on my bedroom ceiling.

"It's been a while since I had a three-way in here," I joked and garnered zero reaction from either one.

"In that closet behind you, there's a shoe rack." I nodded to the closet door. "If you could just grab a pair of shoes for me, please."

Tyler opened the closet door and tossed a pair of shoes to me. I thought for just a nanosecond about making a joke along the lines of having a butler, but figured it might be better to take the stairs back down to the first floor, rather than being thrown out the window.

"Could you hand me my wallet and cellphone, there on top of the dresser?"

"You really think you'll need them?"

"Just in case." I smiled.

Tyler grunted and tossed them on my bed.

"Okay, all set, I guess," I said, shoving the wallet and phone in my pockets, attempting to sound agreeable.

"Not quite, just one more accessory," Baby Face said, and pulled his handcuffs off his belt.

"Hey, look, guys, that isn't necessary."

"Procedure," Tyler said, putting an end to any further discussion.

Baby Face turned me around and pulled my hands behind my back forcefully, but not overly so.

A minute later, we were standing out on my front porch, Tyler, Baby Face, and me. My hands were cuffed behind my back. Tyler pulled the door closed and locked it with my key. The two patrolmen that had been posted at my back door were walking down the driveway toward the street. They looked like they lifted weights for a living, and being cops was maybe just a side job. I wondered what all these muscled cops meant for the doughnut business in town.

"Problems?" one asked.

"No, the picture of respectability." Baby Face laughed.

"You sure you got the right guy?"

Selby Avenue, my street, was busy with lots of traffic. It was the main route for the 21A Selby to Lake Street bus. But today, no one driving past seemed to pay attention to me standing there in handcuffs. Apparently, my being arrested had become a regular occurrence.

An older neighbor lady I'd seen many times before slowly walked past with her dog, little, with curly white hair, the dog that is. She was swathed in a paisley tent affair. Her hair had been dyed a shocking shade of red. Her rouged cheeks seemed to flush with even more color as she glared at me.

"Good morning." I smiled. Tyler and Baby Face were on either side of me, holding my handcuffed arms as we marched down the porch steps.

"Oh, I'm not surprised in the least," she growled. As she spoke, she shook a plastic bag full of dog shit at me then beat a hasty retreat along the sidewalk.

"You always have that effect on women?" Officer Tyler asked.

I couldn't help but think this total waste of taxpayer money seemed to be an overreaction to the assault charge Emma Bitch had no doubt gone ahead and filed. I thought it best to wait until I was officially charged before I called Louie, my lawyer. He'd mention the withdrawal of seventeen witness statements, and we'd see where things went from there.

Twenty-two

We were seated in interview room number three. A trendy little affair, if grey cinderblock walls and damp air conditioning holding just the hint of nervous sweat was your thing.

I had been left sitting in there for close to two hours. In the past thirty minutes, I'd been joined by Louie Laufen, my lawyer. I was still handcuffed, although the cuffs were no longer behind my back.

"Oh, God," Louie half burped, then screwed the top back onto a blue plastic Maalox bottle. "I don't know what I ate last night."

"A bottle of Jim Beam from the smell of that burp," I said. "Louie, can we get back to the matter at hand here?" I said, then raised my handcuffed wrists as a gentle reminder.

"Oh yeah, sure Dev, just not quite a hundred percent today, that's all."

"Great."

I had no doubt Manning was probably watching through the two way mirrors on the wall behind Louie. He was probably one of a number of them, all enjoying the little fun-fest they were having at my expense.

"So, tell me again," Louie said, burping more bourbon fumes. He looked down at the half-page of notes he'd scribbled on the yellow legal pad.

"It was the halftime. The girls all came into the locker room all pissed off, swearing, then Emma—"

"Real name Felicity Bard, correct?"

"Yeah, correct. Then Emma begins slamming her helmet against one of the lockers, again and again. She seems to be the most pissed off, says something about kicking a red-headed American bitch's ass."

"Typical locker room stuff," Louie said.

"Pretty much. My point is she, Emma, seems the most pissed off."

"Then what happens?"

"Jimmy, their security guy, calls me out into the hall, the girls come out maybe ten minutes later, and Emma goes nuts on me. I defend myself, and then they keep her overnight for observation in Regions Hospital. At the request of my contact—"

"This Justine woman?"

"Yeah. She asks me to call Jimmy McNaughton, arrange to meet and try and smooth things over with Emma."

"Now, as far as you know, at this point, all the statements regarding the incident in the hallway have been withdrawn?"

"Yeah, well except for Emma's. So, I apologized to her then as I'm leaving, she yells she still might file charges, and here I am. Apparently, she wasn't joking about filing charges."

"Sounds like the proverbial slam dunk," Louie said.

"I can only hope."

With that, the door opened. At no surprise Detective Norris Manning came in, bald head shining pink. He attacked the always present piece of gum with his front teeth, cracking it as he approached. There were two other people behind him. One I maybe recognized, a guy about forty, curly salt and pepper hair. He was wearing a sport coat and loose tie. He had one of those five-o'clock shadows some guys permanently have and dark bags beneath his eyes. I couldn't put a name to him.

The other individual was a woman, attractive in a tough-looking, no-nonsense way. She wore black slacks and an off white blouse. She was blonde, with a tight jawline and a nice figure. She had very dark eyebrows and brown eyes I guessed the drapes probably didn't match the rug.

"Mr. Haskell, Mr. Laufen," Manning said, sitting down, laying a file on the table in front of him.

I nodded.

"Detective Manning," Louie answered.

"This is Detective Franco, Detective Schumacher," Manning introduced his accomplices.

Franco rang a bell, that was the name. I'd worked with him on a lottery scam a couple of years back, met for all of twenty minutes. Schumacher, the no-nonsense woman, I'd never seen before. Both nodded as Manning said their name, then took up positions leaning against the wall.

"Where to begin, where to begin," Manning said, making a dramatic act of opening a file and then giving a long sigh.

"Maybe you could begin with the charge against my client," Louie said.

"Or the withdrawal of seventeen sworn statements," I added.

Louie gave me a look suggesting I should just be quiet, but I knew better and decided I was going to enjoy this.

"You know as well as I do that this is bullshit, Manning."

"Dev," Louie cautioned.

"Ask any of those English girls."

"Dev."

"Ask their security guy, Jimmy McNaughton. Ask any of the Bombshells."

"Dev, stop it."

"Go ahead, ask Fiona Simmons, the one they call, Harlotte Davidson, she'll tell you that I—"

"God damn it, Dev, shut up," Louie yelled.

"Yes, if I could just get a word in edgewise here. I mean, we're all interested in what you have to say, Mr. Haskell. No, really we are. It's just that, well, in order to check with Miss Simmons well, I'd love to, but someone firebombed her hotel room, and she's in the hospital right now."

"Hospital?" Louie and I answered in unison then stared wide eyed at Manning.

Twenty-three

We'd been in the interview room for a number of hours, to be honest, it felt like weeks. Franco and Schumacher hadn't done so much as blink. In fact, they'd done nothing other than lean against the wall and occasionally adjust positions. That was okay with me. Manning had been piling it on just fine without help from anyone.

"Difficult as it may seem to believe this, I'm still having a problem with your story," Manning said to me.

"So let me get this straight, you told Miss Justine Dahl that you intended to, and I quote, 'Light a fire under that bitch's ass', referring to Miss Bard. Is that correct? Are those your words? Light a fire under that bitch's ass?"

"Well, yeah, I might have said something like that, maybe, but it was just a phrase."

"And during the same phone conversation, you suggested to Justine Dahl that Felicity Bard was in your words a real bitch? Is that correct?"

"No, not exactly. See Miss Bard's roller derby name is Emma Babe, E-M-M-A." I spelled it out. "I was just doing a little clever play on words. You know suggesting it should be Emma Bitch, see? I was just making a little joke."

"A little joke?" Manning asked.

"Well, maybe more to make a point," I said before Louie could stop me.

I think I was the only one in the room who got the play on words.

"So then to add to the joke, to make your point, you firebombed the hotel room of Fiona Simmons and Felicity Bard."

"No."

"Miss Simmons is hospitalized, and Miss Bard has been released and is recovering, again. A hundred and fifty hotel guests were evacuated, just so you could *make your point* as you say."

"Look, I said the things you have there in your file. I'm not denying that fact. But it's a huge jump to go from that…" I nodded at his file. "…to firebombing a hotel room. Don't you think?"

"No, not really, Mr. Haskell, not really."

"I didn't do this," I said.

"And you commented to Mr. James McNaughton that you noticed there was no security present at the hotel room, is that correct?"

"Yes, yeah, I said that. But, only because Jimmy had told me, they were going to hire hotel staff to remain round the clock outside that hotel room. When I saw no one was posted outside Felicity's room, I questioned it. I didn't think it was a good idea."

"Questioned it in order to see just how that might work to your benefit?"

"No, I questioned it because he had told me differently, that's all. I felt they should have security posted outside the room."

"Did you view that as a lost business opportunity, Mr. Haskell?"

"Lost business opportunity?"

"That's what I said. Guarding the room, wasn't that a lost opportunity for you? Work you apparently missed out on."

"No, no, I didn't think anything like that."

"You weren't upset they hadn't hired you to provide security at the hotel?"

"No, I just told you, I wondered why they had removed their security. Jimmy said it was because of budgetary cutbacks."

"Yeah, their whole budget went to hell after you assaulted Miss Bard, didn't it?"

"Sharp observation, except I didn't assault her. But, their budget was getting pretty tight, I gathered, so anyway it was an expense they apparently decided to do without."

"Yes, apparently. Too bad, isn't it?"

Twenty-four

I was prepared to spend the night in a cell. But, some-how, Louie convinced them I wasn't a flight risk, and besides, Manning didn't charge me. It was after seven when we got out of the interview room. We were standing outside on Kellogg Boulevard, which, even af-ter rush hour traffic was still backed up. The drivers all had that bumper-to-bumper look on their face

"Let me drop you off at home," Louie said.

"Thanks, I could use a shower, and I'd just like to forget the day."

"Yeah, you aren't kidding."

"Hey, you're getting paid to be in there. How tough can it be?" I asked.

"No, I meant you could use a shower."

Louie gave me a lift home in his rust accented blue Nissan Sentra. In case I thought the holding cell and the interview room had been bad, Louie's car put all that to shame. I had my window down in an attempt to get some air moving over the trash and debris fluttering around the inside of his car.

"No offense, Louie, but your car could use a shov-eling out and then a pretty aggressive decontamination."

"Huh?"

"You kidding? You've got Big Mac wrappers with Christmas wreaths printed on them blowing around the back seat and its summer. I'm sure I wouldn't have to search very hard to find a couple of empty bottles under the seat. I see at least three Domino's boxes. I didn't know they even delivered to cars. All the unopened mail back there, this one's from the power company," I said and pulled a brown envelope edged in red from a random pile. Red block letters above the address window read 'Open Immediately.'

"What the hell is that?" Louie asked.

"I've gotten these myself from time to time. It's a shut-off notice from Xcel Energy."

"Not to worry, I paid that one, months ago," he said.

"Great, but that doesn't make your car less of a rolling dumpster. God forbid you ever have the opportunity to chauffeur around someone worthwhile."

"You mean as opposed to you?"

"Exactly," I said.

We were heading up Kellogg, turning left just past the History Center at the top of the hill, then right at the Cathedral and down Selby with the sun in our eyes. I'd be home in three blocks. After my day being interrogated and now Louie's car, I was debating if I should toss my clothes in the trash or just burn them as hazardous waste.

"Oh, oh," Louie said, pulling up in front of my place. He ground a good quarter inch off the side of his tires rolling against the curb before he came to a stop.

Crime scene tape crisscrossed the front door, yellow tape, maybe four inches wide with large black letters, all capitals, CRIME SCENE DO NOT CROSS. There was a red notice taped to the inside of the glass on my front door. I could read the heading from the street.

No Admittance
By order of the Saint Paul Police Department

"Are you kidding me?" I said.

"Doesn't look like anyone's kidding."

"That Goddamn Manning. He knew about this," I said. "This is his idea of a joke."

"I'd say he's got a pretty lousy sense of humor. What'd you ever do to him?" Louie asked, shaking his head.

"I've no idea, believe me."

Crime scene tape crisscrossed my double garage, and there were two more red notices taped to the garage door just in case I missed one.

Fortunately, I'd been deliberately over-served the night before, and rather than thread a path up my drive-way, I'd parked at the curb across the street.

"You need a place to land tonight?" Louie asked. "I got a recliner," he said, still staring at the yellow tape fluttering against my front door.

"Thanks, but I'll be okay." I'd spent a night or two in Louie's recliner. Before I ever did that again, I'd stake out a park bench.

"You sure?"

"Positive."

"I'll call you tomorrow, see what we can do to get this place opened up for you," Louie said, but didn't sound all that sure.

"Yeah, you bet."

"Come on, it won't be that bad, we'll get it worked out. Sure you don't need a place to land tonight?"

I nodded and then groaned as I crawled out of Louie's passenger door. I stuck my head back in the window.

"Thanks for the help today, Louie. I'll call you tomorrow."

"Take care, man," Louie said. As he accelerated down the street, a bluish cloud of exhaust rolled up around me and drifted down the street into the setting sun.

I decided there was no point wasting time calling Justine. So I phoned Carol hoping that French guy had dumped her by now and I could scam a place with benefits to stay for the night. She answered almost immediately.

"Oui," she said, sounding just a little too cheery.

"Hi, Carol, Dev Haskell."

"Oh." She suddenly sounded decidedly colder and followed up with a long pause. I blinked first.

"Just checking in, wondered if you were doing anything tonight."

"I'd appreciate it if you wouldn't call me again, ever," she said, then hung up.

I tried Kristi, but my cell displayed a 'number blocked' message.

Naomi's number had been changed, with no further information available.

I left a message for Patti, but she was probably still pissed off about the little cigar burn I left on her great-grandmother's heirloom dining room table. I didn't hold out much hope.

I reluctantly phoned Heidi Bauer. I didn't want to, but I was pretty much out of options.

"Hello." She sounded happy.

"Hi, Heidi, Dev."

"Yeah," she said, suddenly sounding cautious.

"Hey, I realize it's pretty short notice, but I was just checking to see what you're up to tonight."

"What I'm up to? Really? You mean you don't want something, bail money, a ride somewhere?"

"Man, when did you become so cynical?"

"Oh, I don't know, maybe after getting you out of a half dozen different jams, posting bail, retrieving various cars from the impound lot, hiding you from the authori-ties…sooner or later even I start to catch on," she said.

"Look, I know it's late. I've just been working a lot, had a halfway open night, wondered if you wanted to get together, that's all. If it's going to present a problem, I can call another time." I hoped I didn't sound too desperate.

"I suppose you'd expect a late dinner?" she said, softening.

"Actually, I was thinking I would pick something up. What do you feel like?"

Twenty-five dollars worth of Chinese take-out and four bottles of wine later, I pulled up in front of Heidi's. She opened the front door as I came up the walk.

"Well, at least you parked in front, so apparently you're not hiding this time."

"Why do you think there has to be something wrong before I want to come over and see you? Can't you just accept the fact I enjoy your company? I thought maybe spending an evening listening to your conversation would be reward enough."

"Yeah, that's what you're after, my conversation."

"That might be part of it . . . find out what you've been up to, who you're seeing, when—"

"Just stop. I'll figure it out sooner or later, and you'll be busted, but for right now, come on in. Pork fried rice, right?" She blocked the doorway and nodded at the grocery bag full of little white containers.

"And dim sum," I added.

"Okay, get your ass in here," she said, stepping aside.

As was our custom, we ate directly out of the containers. Heidi ate all her dim sum then moved on to mine. I made a point of never letting her glass go empty. She had finished the better part of three bottles of wine when she attempted to make grasshoppers for dessert. That didn't work so well under the circumstances, so we moved on to the bedroom course.

Twenty-five

Heidi groaned from under her pillow. "Oh, God, what kind of cheapo wine was that? My head's killing me."

"Couldn't have been the three bottles you had," I said.

"You were drinking, too."

"I had a glass to every one of your bottles. That was before you decided to make the grasshoppers."

"Grasshoppers?"

She lounged in bed, groaning for another forty minutes, working up the courage to face the day. I tried to get something romantic happening with the proverbial back rub, but it didn't work. Eventually we climbed out of bed and wandered out of her bedroom.

My clothes were scattered around the living room. As I pulled on my jeans, I heard Heidi in the kitchen.

"God, I don't remember any of this," she said. She was standing naked in the middle of the room. You could tell she was running through her memory files, and they were all coming up blank. Even hungover, she still looked beautiful.

I couldn't say that much for the kitchen. Almost a dozen little white take-out containers littered the granite countertop. Bits of rice were scattered here and there, a half-eaten dim sum. There were two wine glasses, one was still partially full, and the other, sporting a half moon of lipstick, had been drained dry. Three empty wine bottles stood on a distant counter next to the refrigerator, while the fourth lay on its side and had rolled up against the microwave, barely a swallow left inside. We had left the ice cream out on the kitchen counter, next to her underwear.

Heidi stared at a puddle of melted ice cream that had dripped onto the kitchen floor. The blender had a green glop sitting in it, and judging from the spray pattern across the kitchen wall, she must have run the thing with the top off.

"Not to worry, you made up for it in the bedroom," I said.

"Apparently. Want some breakfast?" she said, placing an aspirin bottle on the kitchen counter then filling a glass up at the refrigerator tap.

"What have you got for breakfast?" I asked.

"I don't know, any of that pork fried rice left?"

Unless we planned on eating puffed rice cakes and melted ice cream, I knew better than to check for any food in her house.

"I'll go get us something. How's that sound?"

"And a Latte, a double," she pleaded.

I was driving back from the coffee shop, armed with four caramel rolls and Heidi's double Latte when my cellphone rang.

"Haskell In…"

"Where the hell have you been, dipshit?"

"Mom?" I asked.

"I've been trying to call you for the past hour and a half," Louie said.

"Sorry, I was in a meeting," I said, thinking I should have checked my phone when I pulled my jeans on.

"Sure you were. Listen as your attorney, let me state, I don't want to know. I spoke with the good Detective Manning about your place."

"And?"

"And, with any luck, they'll finish up, and you can get back in there by the end of the day."

"Fantastic."

"Just keep your fingers crossed."

When I returned, Heidi had progressed to one of the couches in her living room. She lay curled up on her living room couch, wearing a pair of sunglasses with a white terrycloth robe wrapped around her. An open can of 7-Up sat within reach on the coffee table.

"Did you remember my Latte?" she groaned from the couch.

"Yeah, a double, and some caramel rolls."

"Mmm-mmm, give me," she pleaded.

I set the Latte in front of her and went out to the kitchen for some plates. Nothing had changed except a half glass of water sat on the counter next to the ice cream container and the open aspirin bottle. Melted ice cream was still pooled on the floor. Her thong from last night rested next to the toaster. I put two caramel rolls on a plate and brought them out to her, then ventured back into the kitchen and started to clean things up.

It took the better part of an hour, but everything was pretty much back to normal. Well, except for the green blender spray across the kitchen wall. That would have to be repainted. I grabbed a shower, then peeked back into the living room. Heidi was asleep on the couch, snoring softly behind her sunglasses. Latte was dribbled down the front of her robe, and only a few caramel crumbs remained on her plate. I knew better than to disturb her and tiptoed out.

Twenty-six

I drove past my house, taking a roundabout way to the office, just to see if I could learn anything. I didn't. A few miles worth of yellow crime scene tape was still wrapped around my house and garage. The place looked like the site of some demented high school prank. There was a white Crime Scene van parked in my driveway with a city logo on the door, but I didn't see anyone outside. With any luck, they'd already finished and were relaxing down the block having coffee at Nina's. I figured it was the wise move to just keep heading toward the office.

It was later that afternoon, and I was eating a platter of Bar-B-Q ribs at a place called Fat Daddy's just around the corner from the office. The tiny room had three small card tables, and maybe a dozen folding chairs with 'First Baptist Church' stenciled across the back. There was an aged poster of Little Anthony and the Imperials held to one of the walls with yellowed tape. A more recent Otis Redding poster, maybe just thirty years old, was taped above the order counter. The air conditioner was either broken or turned off, and the place smelled of my sweat and sweet, tangy Bar-B-Q grease.

With the exception of Fat Daddy, all four-hundred-and–fifty-pounds of him sweating behind the cash register, I was the only person in the place. Fat Daddy was sipping something from a travel mug. I guessed it wasn't a Diet-Coke. I could hear the ice cubes rattle whenever he sipped. He hadn't said much more than 'What'll you have?' since I'd entered the place twenty minutes earlier.

My cellphone rang.

"Haskell…"

"Where are you?" Louie interrupted.

"My office. You hear anything from Manning yet?"

"Where exactly, are you?"

"Exactly? Okay, I'm grabbing some ribs just around the corner at Fat Daddy's. Why, is there a problem?"

"If they're not there yet, some of the city's finest are on their way to pay you a personal visit."

"Now what?"

"I haven't been informed. My guess? They found something during their search of your place."

"There was nothing to find."

"You sure?"

"Yeah, Louie, honest, there was nothing. Look, they come up with drugs or something, it's a plant. I'm not kidding. They find any money they have to split it with me."

Louie didn't react to my joke.

"Think you can get to your car?"

I looked out through the second 'B' in Fat Daddy's three-foot high, hand-painted B-B-Q letters on his front window. My car sat across the street, parked at the curb, minding its own business maybe thirty feet from the corner.

"Yeah, I can see my car from here."

"You should be on your feet and moving now. You got two, maybe three minutes tops. I want you to meet me downtown at the police station."

"What?"

"We're going to turn you in, do the upstanding citizen thing, answer whatever questions they have and hopefully move on. You're sure there's nothing there, at your place?"

"Yeah, I'm sure, there's absolutely nothing there unless they're looking for laundry."

"Unregistered guns, drugs, kiddie porn?"

"No, nothing, honest…maybe some vacation photos of naked women, but…"

"Are they over eighteen?"

"Yes, they're over eighteen."

"Good, meet me at the cop shop. You know that parking lot, the one across the street?"

"Yeah."

"Don't screw around, Dev. I'm talking a couple of minutes here, that's all you got."

I pushed back from the card table and walked out the door.

"Gotta run, Fatty," I called over my shoulder

"You coming back, Dev?" Fat Daddy called after me. He never got off his stool behind the cash register.

I turned the key in the ignition and took a right at the corner. I hadn't driven more than thirty seconds when I saw a flashing light turn onto Randolph maybe three blocks further down coming toward me, fast. I pulled to the side, giving the police car plenty of room. It was a dark blue Crown Victoria, with a removable light flashing on top, no siren, just like on TV. Franco was driving, Manning sat in the passenger seat, and I could tell he was chewing gum. They shot past me, and I watched them in my rearview mirror. A black and white came off a side street and pulled in behind them. They parked going against traffic, right in front of the stairs leading up to my office. They jumped out of their cars and left the flashing lights on. That was enough for me. I pulled away from the curb and went to meet Louie.

I had been baking in the parking lot for close to an hour, watching as the heat shimmered off the hood of my car. The lot was two acres of weeds and graveled pot-holes completely devoid of shade. Every time a car drove through the lot, another layer of choking yellow dust sifted down onto me and the other parked vehicles fading beneath the unrelenting sun.

Louie's Sentra finally scraped up the entry and across the sidewalk, then wheezed into a spot next to the sign that warned drivers 'Do not leave your vehicle un-attended.' Not exactly a ringing endorsement for the po-lice station across the street.

"Where the hell have you been?" I asked, drifting through a cloud of blue exhaust. Louie had turned his car off, but it continued to rattle and shudder for another fifteen seconds, before completely shutting down altogether in a mild explosion.

"Trying to figure out what they've got cooked up for us," he groaned as he climbed out from behind the wheel.

He wore what used to be a light blue suit. The trousers looked permanently wrinkled, and there was some kind of brownish sauce dribbled down the lapel on the right side of his coat. He attempted to straighten his tie, but only managed to position it slightly more off-center. The top button of his shirt was undone, but his chins managed to hide the fact. Darker sweat stains began to seep through the underarms of his suit coat.

"Might as well see what they've got on you," he said, heading across the street in the direction of the police station. He was wheezing heavily before he made it to the far curb.

I watched for a moment, then I hurried to catch up in the event he needed help crossing the street.

"Maybe you should find out what's up and call me, rather than bringing me in there and—"

"Let's just go in there and let them know you've got nothing to hide. I'm sure there's a logical explanation for whatever it is they found."

Twenty-seven

I was moving up in the world. This time we were in Interview Room Number One. Its décor was remarkably similar to the previous interview room, charmless grey cinder block walls with a video camera hanging from the ceiling in one corner. The green light was on, indicating I was being filmed. The back wall had two-way mirrors mounted the entire length, and I gathered we were playing to an audience. There was a scent in the room mixed with the damp air conditioning and most likely emanating from me, fear, desperation, and panic.

Detectives Manning and Franco were in the room sitting across from Louie and me. Between us was a grey Formica table whose only feature was a couple of cigarette burns snaking their way toward the chipped edge.

There were a dozen different photos strewn across the table in front of us, each one a slightly different image of the finger they'd found while searching my garage. It was a severed middle finger, with the fingertip hacked off.

The thing had been wrapped in a plastic bag and placed in a small refrigerator that stood in the back of my garage. Based on the photos, I guessed the thing was decomposed. Substantially decomposed.

"For the thousandth time, I'm telling you I have no idea how in the hell that thing got in my garage. I sure as hell didn't put it there."

"Haskell, do you mean to say you forgot you left that finger in your garage?" Franco asked. He'd been the good cop for the past hour, or was it two hours?

"No. I'm saying I've never seen that thing before. I never put it in my garage."

"Why did you keep the finger in that refrigerator?" Manning asked.

"So I could give you one, the finger, that is."

"Dev," Louie cautioned.

"Look, I don't know how the thing got there, okay? If I was storing a bunch of fingers, would I put them in a refrigerator that hasn't worked in over two years? If you guys bothered to check, you would have noticed the thing was unplugged. It's been unplugged for at least two years. Someone is setting me up here."

"So you admit you were storing a number of fingers. Was this the last one?"

"I don't admit anything of the sort. I just told you the refrigerator doesn't work. It's been broken for a couple of years. If it did work, I would have had beer in it."

"Let's go back to the night you firebombed the hotel room," Manning said.

"I didn't firebomb anything."

Manning was up and walking back and forth across the room, playing to the audience behind the mirrors. As he walked, he absently stretched and twisted the rubber band that had held the photos of the fingers.

"So you go to the hotel and—"

"I didn't firebomb any hotel room."

"You stated you were intoxicated that night."

"No, as a matter of fact, I said I was very intoxicated that night. So much so that I parked on the street, because I didn't want to attempt driving down my narrow driveway and into my garage."

"And you left The Spot bar sometime after two that morning."

"That's what I'm told."

"So you drove to the hotel, firebombed the hotel room of Felicity Bard and Fiona Simmons, then drove home and decided to park on the street?"

"No, I left The Spot. I drove home. I parked on the street and then went to bed."

"To sleep?"

"Okay, have it your way, I decided to read for a few hours. No, like I've been telling you, I more or less passed out. And I did not firebomb any hotel room."

"You phoned a number of different departments impersonating a police officer from Saint Paul. Is that correct, Mr. Haskell?"

"No. I phoned a number of different police departments. When they asked me if you were as big an asshole as you seemed. I said, yes. If that makes it sound like I'm a member of the Saint Paul department, there really isn't much I can do about it."

Manning had walked to the far end of the room and snapped the rubber band he'd been stretching, then turned and looked at me.

"You did call a number of different departments, did you not?"

"I did, four to be exact. Denver, St. Louis, Chicago, and Kansas City. At no time did I tell anyone I was a member of the Saint Paul Police Department. If the individuals I spoke with arrived at that conclusion, it was on their own."

"Why did you call?"

"I've told you. Jimmy McNaughton had hired me to help with security. I was attempting to learn anything we could about the fingers that had been sent to the Hastings Hustlers."

"He didn't feel the police could give adequate protection, so he thought he better go right to the top, meaning you. That right?"

"More like he had you as his point of contact with the department, Manning. I'm sure after your standard confidence-building speech regarding budget cuts. He figured even I didn't sound half bad."

"What was it like doing the security for that English team? Did I hear right? You were in their locker room?" Franco asked, playing good cop.

"Yeah. You know, it was just a job, comes with the territory. Twenty or so gorgeous naked women and all of them trying to get my attention, what you might call just an average day's work."

Manning flushed close to purple.

"That why you attacked the Bard woman? What is she about five-one, a hundred pounds?"

"I didn't attack anyone."

"We've sworn statements."

"Actually no, you don't, Detective. I believe all, but one of those statements has been withdrawn. The one remaining statement is from Miss Bard herself, hardly credible in the face of sixteen statements being withdrawn," Louie said.

"You scare off all those little English girls, Haskell?"

"Don't answer that, Dev," Louie said. "I wonder if I might have a moment with my client, Detective?"

Manning and Franco nodded almost in unison. Franco got up from his chair.

"Ten minutes enough time?" Manning asked, suddenly the voice of reason.

"Ten minutes will be perfect," Louie said then watched the two of them depart the interview room.

Louie turned to me and moved his eyes to indicate the mirrored wall, reminding me we were not entirely alone.

After ten or twenty thousand hours of questioning, I felt completely drained. I was definitely in need of a serious shower. Louie, on the other hand, had arrived in that state, but right now, he seemed to look better than me, a lot better. I couldn't recall what exactly we had been discussing and suddenly came back to reality.

". . . seems to be finally going our way," Louie said.

"Huh? Going our way? You're delusional. You gotta be kidding."

"In my opinion, you've been set up. God knows why."

There was a knock on the door, and Manning poked his head in.

"Ready to continue? Need a coffee or anything?" he asked, again sounding the voice of reason.

Louie waved him in. "Let's just get this finished up as quickly as possible."

Manning went over the same ground all over again, and again, and again.

Finally, I couldn't stand anymore.

"You know what you should do, Manning? You should check my place out for DNA related to the fingers that were mailed to those other cities. I'd haul that refrigerator of mine from my garage into your lab, see if you can find anything. Maybe check the post mark on those envelopes. Run the things for a DNA comparison with me. Something's bound to come together for you guys."

"We're already doing that." He smiled.

"You're catching on," I said.

"Detective, is there any new ground you wanted to cover?" Louie asked. "Because if there isn't, I really think Mr. Haskell has been more than cooperative, wouldn't you agree?"

"I agree we've most likely covered enough ground for today, Mr. Laufen," Manning said to Louie, but he continued to stare at me.

"Then I take it you are about to charge Mr. Haskell? Or are we free to go?" Louie asked.

Charge me? I looked at Louie, wide-eyed.

"For the time being, you are free to go," Manning said.

Twenty-eight

The crime scene tape was still keeping me out of my place. I didn't think I possessed the stamina to spend a second night at Heidi's. I was sitting in my car, wondering who I could possibly call and scam an overnight from when my cellphone rang.

"Haskell Investigations."

"Hello, Dev, it's Carol," she said, sounding sultry.

Well, surprise, surprise, if it wasn't little Miss Pepe Le Pew.

"Hi, Carol, nice to hear from you. Wow, I'm a little surprised."

"Surprised?"

"Yeah, the last time we spoke, yesterday I think, you told me never to call you again. It's really nice to hear your voice. How have you been?" I figured I'd better soft-peddle it since I needed a place to stay. Carol and her implanted attributes could be just the thing the doctor ordered.

"Dev, you're so sweet. Things have been positively wonderful. I can't thank you enough for introducing Nicholas to me."

"Introducing Nicholas? Carol, I didn't introduce the two of you. We were out on a date, you and me. I was attempting to ply you with Cosmopolitans if you'll re-call. Then that Nicholas guy showed up and took my stool, and the next thing, I know you're speaking French."

"Oh, don't be silly. It's just that he is so different, so interesting, so, so, romantic. He's, oh, I don't knon, so really different than you. I mean, in a number of good ways, I guess."

That didn't really help me.

"And he's been such a little gentleman."

I didn't want to touch the 'little' line. I was hoping maybe Pepe Le Pew was out of town, and Carol was fishing for a little ungentlemanly behavior on my part.

"What can I do for you? Maybe we should get to…"

"Just a tiny favor I'd like to ask."

I quickly ran the list of her particular perversions through my mind.

"How can I help?" I said, then checked my face in the rearview mirror.

"I left a couple of Leonard Cohen CDs at your place. Any chance you could run them over tonight? Nicholas will be here sometime after…"

I decided it wouldn't be the best idea to tell her I'd tossed them both in the trash. You'd slit your wrists be-fore you finished listening to one CD from that guy, let alone both of them, totally depressing.

"…to prepare a special night."

"I'd love to get them to you Carol but I can't."

"Can't or won't," she shot back, her charming attitude suddenly gone.

"Look, I'd like nothing better than to help with your love life, but I can't get them tonight."

"Out with some bar floozy?"

"I only wish. No, I—"

She hung up. So much for Carol providing me comfort for the night.

Against my better judgment, I found myself on the front porch, ringing Louie's doorbell less than an hour later. It was a muggy, dreadfully still evening, and the two front windows at Louie's house were open with large fans roaring and clattering. The storm door stood open in a failed attempt to collect whatever breeze there wasn't. I rang the front doorbell again, then heard the thing chime from somewhere inside. Further back in the house, I could hear a woman's voice. She sounded like she was pleading. Whoever it was, she was in trouble.

"Hello?" I called and then heard a shriek. I pulled on the screen door, but it was hooked. I pulled hard, wrenched the thing open, and tore a part of the door as I did, splitting the wood where the hook had been a moment before. I followed the woman's shrieks down the hall. Louie was in his den, snoring in his ratty recliner, close to a dozen beer bottles scattered around him on the floor. He was passed out in front of his flat screen. On screen, two women screamed as they tested the support system on a tandem bicycle that careened down a steep, winding hill.

I walked into the kitchen and helped myself to a cold bottle of Summit from his fridge, then returned to Louie's den. I lifted the remote from the arm of his recliner, settled into an equally ratty couch, and started flicking through channels until I found a movie I'd only seen three or four times.

Louie woke me sometime after midnight.

"Want another beer?" he asked, holding a cold bottle out in my general direction.

"Thanks."

"No woman out there stupid enough to put up with you tonight?" he asked, and then followed up by chugging almost a third of his beer.

I shook my head.

"Any idea who put that thing in your garage?"

"Someone who doesn't know me very well. Just about everyone knew that little fridge was dead. And if they didn't, once they opened it up, they should have gotten the hint."

"Hint?" he asked, then chugged another third.

"You kidding? I had boxes of nails and screws in there. What kind of idiot sees that stuff in a refrigerator and then decides to toss a finger in?"

"I don't know. Some guy in a hurry, worried about getting caught sneaking in or rushing out. Someone who doesn't really care, someone who wants to set you up, see you get jacked around and nailed."

"The guy sees the fridge. First of all, he has to move a bunch of shit just to get to the thing. He opens it up. The light doesn't go on, it's not cold. There's boxes of hardware in there, a couple of paint cans, seems like a pretty weak set up to me."

"Maybe." Louie drained his bottle and didn't ask if I wanted another. He just walked back into the kitchen and reappeared thirty seconds later with two more beers. He handed one to me. I set it down on the floor.

"Plus, are you telling me the guy who was stalking Harlotte Davidson all this time around the country was some moron from Saint Paul?" I asked.

"That second part, being a moron…that seems pretty plausible."

"Yeah, that's for sure. But hell, I didn't even know these English roller derby gals existed until Justine put me in touch with them."

"Well, there you go. Obviously, if the great Dev Haskell didn't know anything about their fundraising tour across the United States, no one else did, either. It just couldn't be news, right?"

I took his point, shrugged my shoulders.

Louie shook his head.

"It's someone connected to the Hasting Hustlers in some way. Some creep has the hots for that Harlotte chick, or she gave some idiot the finger, and now he's following her around. What do they call it when all those creeps follow Jodie Foster around? It's probably something like that," Louie said.

"What do they call it? Nuts, is what they call it. They're all whack jobs. But, I'm still not sure that explains the finger."

"The one in your garage?"

I nodded and took a sip.

"I honestly think it's a diversion."

"Gee, really? You mean some douche bag didn't just walk around and pick up a middle finger lying on the sidewalk? Then decided to hide the thing in my garage?"

"Yeah, I know it didn't *just* happen. The thing is obviously from the guy who's really been doing this shit. Otherwise, it makes absolutely no sense at all."

"Makes no sense, you mean unlike everything else so far?" I said.

"I'm only half-joking here when I say at no surprise you must have pissed someone off. You might want to think about who it could be."

"That list is long," I said, then drained my bottle of beer and grabbed the fresh one off the floor.

Twenty-nine

I was finally allowed back into my house late the next day. Manning had been right. They did take the non-working refrigerator from the garage. They also took the working refrigerator from my kitchen, along with all my knives, my toolbox, a table saw, a skill saw, and strangely, a set of utensils for eating lobster that I'd gotten as a Christmas gift some years back and never used. The things were still in the original box.

All the stuff that had been kept in my refrigerator; butter, oranges, leftover pizza, cranberry juice, doggy bags from restaurants, ice cube trays, all of it had been scattered across my kitchen counter. The beer was missing. Nothing was left out that twenty-four hours in humid weather wouldn't help make worse. It was the second time that week I'd cleaned up a gallon of melted ice cream. I bagged everything and threw it all in the trash, then opened the windows to air the place out.

Louie phoned later that evening. I could hear glasses clinking and the low hum of background conversation.

"How are you holding up?" he asked.

"I've been worse, but it's been a while."

"They grab that refrigerator?"

"The one in the garage? Yeah. They also took the one in my kitchen, virtually all my tools, my table saw, all my knives. God knows what else."

"Well, I know it's a pain, but it's not like there's anything to find, right?"

"That's what you said before, and then they found that finger in my garage. I don't know, I just want all this over and done with. It sucks big time."

"Mmm-mmm," Louie said after swallowing. "Yeah, not fun. For what it's worth, I got a call from a source over at BCA."

"The crime analysis folks? What'd they have to say?"

"About all they could confirm was they got a finger."

"I could have told them that."

"Nothing from any database, no match. He said it had been frozen before. The finger that is."

"Just like King's," I said absently.

"What?"

"The guy I spoke with in Denver, King Quinn, Kingston, actually. He said they determined the same thing. The finger left there had been frozen. That was the one taped to the door of the bus. They couldn't link it to anything in the CODIS database. Might be worth a heads up to your source, see if they want to contact King. Maybe together they can come up with something, anything."

"Give me his name again," Louie said. "I'm writing it down on a bar napkin. Got a phone number?"

Once we were finished and I'd hung up, Louie's call got me thinking, so I called Andy Lindbergh.

"Hi Andy, Dev Haskell. Sorry to bother you at home."

"No problem, Dev, but if you're calling for bail money, the answer's no," he only half-joked.

"No, they just held me for questioning, but I'm out now. Not fun, let me tell you."

Dead silence on the other end.

"Andy?"

"You serious?"

"Yeah, not to worry. Say, let me ask you something. You were telling me the other day about the crematorium, as maybe a place to harvest."

"You're back on the fingers, right?"

"Yeah. Let me ask you a question. We've gotten results back on two fingers. I'm just guessing, but what are the chances of two random fingers not matching DNA anywhere in our databases?"

"From two different individuals?"

"Most likely," I said.

"Pretty much eliminates the usual suspects."

"Meaning?"

"Meaning the usual suspects, criminals, someone who has been convicted of a felony, sex offenders. You mentioned a bunch of cities, right?"

"Yeah, four. Plus, the latest was here, in St. Paul, so that's actually five, now."

"Okay, the set up varies from state to state, but in general its criminals, your violent offenders, guys guilty of sex crimes. I think in a couple of states, they may have extended it to guys who have been charged but not convicted. Anyway, individuals in that area of the criminal justice system. Based on what you've told me, one would think it's an individual like that involved. But the results, at least initially, don't seem to confirm your supposition."

"Yeah, all CODIS, I get that part. What about other countries?"

"A lot of them have a similar system."

"What about England?"

"The UK?"

"Yeah."

They have a database. Actually, I think their system predates ours and is a little more thorough. I suppose you could theoretically check their system or Interpol or something like that, nab some major international villain. But you'd have to be dealing with a major crime, murders, probably plural. Maybe multiple tons of drugs. I mean, this finger deal with the English roller derby team is weird, but I'm certain it's not even a blip on the screen of international law enforcement," Andy said.

I spent the rest of the night online, looking at illicit dating sites.

Thirty

I checked my bedroom clock as I reached for my cellphone, 7:10 in glowing green numbers.

"Hask…" I had to clear my throat. "Haskell Investigations."

"Gee, sorry, hope I'm not disturbing that much needed beauty sleep of yours," the voice sounded way too cheery and not at all sorry. I heard the gum cracking.

"Detective Manning?"

"I suppose you're already at your desk."

I laid back and let out a long sigh. This couldn't possibly go my way.

"What can I do for you, Detective?"

"Wonder if we might chat, I…"

"Let me get in touch with my attorney."

"I got a better idea. How about I send a car around, say fifteen minutes?"

"Are you going to arrest me again?"

"No, actually Haskell, much as that would make my day, the answer is no. You will not be put under arrest. In fact, we'll be chatting in my office."

"Chatting?"

"Just a few informal questions."

"In your office?"

"Yes. How do you take your coffee."

"Actually, I'm into double Latte's nowadays," I said, hoping to be difficult.

"I'll have a squad there for you in fifteen minutes."

I stumbled downstairs to the kitchen, put some coffee on, then went back up to shower. I had just stepped out of the shower and was toweling off when my doorbell rang. I wrapped the towel around my waist and went downstairs to open the door, figuring Manning had probably sent some more weightlifters bent on intimidation, and they'd break the door in, just for practice.

The bell rang a second time just as I got to the entryway. I saw the back of a blue uniform shirt through the window and opened the door. The officer turned to face me just as I opened door.

"You didn't have to do that for me," she smiled, nodding at the towel wrapped around my waist.

I missed a couple of beats as I stared into the dark brown eyes and gorgeous face of an Asian female. Her eyes held a definite sparkle. I glanced down from her face and stared at the gold thread embroidered over her breast pocket, Trang, L.

"You are Mr. Devlin Haskell, right?" She smiled.

"What?"

"Are you Mr. Devlin Haskell?" As she asked, she stepped back and double-checked the address numbers next to my front door.

"Yes, yes, I'm sorry, officer. I…well, you caught me off guard. Look, I'll be ready in just a minute. I just got Manning's phone call a few minutes ago. Please, please, come in." I stepped back to let her in but decided against asking her upstairs to help me get dressed.

She seemed to consider for a moment, then nodded.

"I guess that would be okay."

"Can I get you a cup of coffee? I just put some on."

"That would be fine," she said and followed me into my kitchen. I sensed her looking around, checking things out as we walked toward the rear of the house. She stared for a moment at the open space my refrigerator used to inhabit. Maybe she noticed the three or four years worth of dust balls that had accumulated. Maybe it was the tops to old beer bottles or the unset, empty mousetrap. If she did notice, she was gracious enough not to say anything.

I pulled a mug out of the cabinet, poured some coffee, and handed it to her.

"Thanks."

"Milk?" I asked, then remembered I didn't have any.

"No, black is fine."

"I'll just get changed upstairs and be back down," I said, pouring a mug for me.

"Take your time, no rush. I'm on the clock." She smiled and sipped.

I had another thought about asking her upstairs to help me pick out the right outfit, then on second thought decided it might not be the best idea and left to get dressed.

I was back downstairs in under eight minutes. Officer L. Trang was leaning against my kitchen counter, next to her empty coffee mug and smiling. She looked me up and down. If she'd been one of my ex's, I thought she might have said something like 'You're not going out dressed like that, are you?' Instead, she just leaned against the counter and continued to smile.

"You know, the last time a police officer was here, I was handcuffed up in my bedroom."

"Really? Interesting," she said, sounding not at all surprised. "Ready to go?"

We were outside, walking down my front steps. The same woman from the other day was just walking past with her little white, curly-haired dog.

"Humpf." She sneered, then shook her head in disgust and stopped to watch us.

"Same day, different shit," I said, nodding at the bag she carried.

"Mr. Haskell," Officer Trang smiled and stood next to the open rear door of the black and white.

"Shouldn't he be handcuffed? He's a menace and a detriment to the entire neighborhood," the old bat said.

"We did that upstairs, used the handcuffs," I said and winked at her.

"Well, hopefully, you'll lose the key when you lock him up this time."

"Yes, Ma-am." Officer Trang said, then closed the door behind me and walked around to the driver's side. She was smiling when she got in behind the wheel.

"I've already been told I have that effect on women."

"Menace and detriment?" she said and started the car.

We were maybe ten minutes from the police station. Not far in terms of distance, but the start and stop of rush hour on streets in a permanent state of construction did nothing to get you where you wanted to go. We hadn't said anything since she pulled away from the front of my house.

"What's the 'L' stand for?" I asked.

"The 'L'?"

"Your first name, it's on your uniform."

"Oh, sorry, it stands for Linh, L-I-N-H," she spelled it out for me.

"Pretty," I said.

"It means gentle spirit," she said.

I waited for her to expound, but nothing else followed. I caught her glancing at me in the rearview mirror a couple of times, probably wracking her brain for 'Wanted' posters.

"My instructions are to escort you up to four," she said, fifteen minutes later. She opened the rear door for me and smiled. We were parked on the street in front of the brick building that served as the police station. We were directly across the street from the dusty, pot-holed lot where I'd waited for Louie the other day.

"Do you want to cuff me?" I asked, then held up my wrists and smiled.

"You'd like that, wouldn't you? No, as a matter of fact, but I was thinking of using the Taser," she replied, then gave a quick laugh and headed for the front door.

Manning was in a burgundy and beige cubicle, seated behind his desk. The cubicle looked ten years old, the scuffed wooden desk closer to fifty. He was half-hidden behind four stacks of thick manila files. The top of his head was a shiny pink outlined by his close-cropped red fringe. When he looked up, his blue eyes were like lasers beaming in on me.

"Any problems, Officer Trang?" he asked, sounding hopeful. Then he cracked his ever-present wad of gum.

"No, he was an absolute model citizen," she said.

"Surprising. I'll call you when we're finished. Sit down, Haskell," Manning directed and indicated a chair for me. The chair was tarnished chrome with olive drab highlights and looked to be army surplus.

I sat down then stared as officer Trang walked back down the hallway in one of the better fitting uniforms I'd seen. I continued to stare, then said to Manning, "I'd tell her anything she wanted to hear."

"Just a word of caution. She's Midwest regional champ three years running in her weight class for kickboxing."

"I'm thinking of the possibilities, maybe just a light spanking," I said.

"You requested a latte," Manning said, ignoring my comment. He reached over the stack of files and handed me a barely lukewarm paper cup, the kind dispensed from a machine. The contents consisted of a creamy coffee-colored sludge with a definite blue oil scum drifting across the top.

"What's this?"

"It passes for a latte down here, or coffee with extra cream and sugar, depending."

"Gee, thanks."

"Don't mention it," Manning said.

"You having anything?"

"You kidding? I wouldn't touch that stuff." He sounded surprised, I even asked.

"So, you wanted to chat, just the two of us," I said, setting the latte or whatever it was on the edge of his desk.

"That's right."

"About?"

"Have you had any contact with the Hastings Hustlers since we last chatted?"

"Last chatted? You've got to be kidding. You can't possibly be referring to the hours of interrogation where you grilled me and my attorney in that stuffy, depressing little room the other day?"

"That might be a little harsh."

"I don't think so. Look, do I have to have him here, my attorney? If I'm going to be charged, I want my attorney present."

"No, I'll level with you. Much as I'd like to nail you, I don't think you did anything, at least not in relation to the Hustlers, those fingers or that firebombing."

"You're kidding?" I was genuinely surprised, shocked might be a better word.

"No, believe me, no one is more disappointed than me, but I'm pretty sure you don't have anything to do with this, other than your usual wrong place at the wrong time which seems to be a pretty routine practice of yours."

"You're saying you believe me when I tell you I'm not involved?"

"At least as far as I can determine at this point."

"Well then, can I have my refrigerator back?"

"I'll see what I can do," he said and penned a quick note across a legal pad.

We sat quietly for a moment, studying the competition across the desk from one another. I finally broke the ice.

"What's going on here, Manning?"

He seemed to size me up, aggressively cracking gum with his front teeth. "Fiona Simmons, Harlotte Davidson, she was murdered last night," he said, and then stared at me.

Thirty-one

I felt the color draining from my face as I said, "I think I should have my attorney present,"

"You're not being charged. You're not even a suspect. Jesus Christ, we've had you under surveillance for the past two days," he said, then threw his pen on the desk.

"Under surveillance?"

"Once again, you haven't failed to disappoint."

"Oh, gee, sorry. Why would you think I had anything to do with this bullshit? She's dead? How? What? She's dead? But she's so nice. I mean—"

"Her roommate found her earlier this morning."

"Earlier?"

"A little after one."

"What was she doing? The roommate, Felicity—"

"Felicity Bard, she was out with a few of the other girls listening to music at some club. Nothing wild or crazy. The Simmons woman was in the hotel after the women left for the club. A number of people saw her. At least four women were with Miss Bard the entire evening."

"She's involved. Emma Babe, the Bard woman, she's involved somehow."

"And you make your living as an investigator? Did you happen to hear anything I just said?"

"Let me guess . . . after all that's been going on they didn't have security outside the door of the room did they?"

"Apparently not."

"Apparently? For God's sake, they got severed fingers being mailed to them across the country. Some maniac firebombed their hotel room. Why in the hell would they possibly pull their security at the— It's because you had me under surveillance, isn't it?

"That has nothing to do with it."

"Jesus Christ, you told them, didn't you? You said I was under surveillance, so they figured it was all over, they were safe. Right?"

"I didn't tell them."

"No? Well, I'm guessing someone did, and they figured they didn't have to worry because the prime suspect, namely me, was essentially under lockdown at home. Right?"

Manning didn't say anything, but his ears looked red, and the top of his head was quickly growing a hotter pink.

"How do you know I didn't sneak out a back window?"

Manning glanced down at the open file in front of him.

"Let's see . . . you made a phone call a little after nine. You were online from about nine-thirty until one-fifteen in the morning. A number of different porn and escort sites. What? Did the word finally get out about you, and now you have to pay for it?" He laughed at his little joke.

"You're paying for it, too, Manning. You just don't know it yet."

"Drunken Mommies, Girls Gone Wild, Back Page, Date Night."

"Okay, okay, I was just looking, which isn't a crime. At least as far as I know."

"Much as I'd like to tie you into this unless you flew up your chimney, over to that hotel on a broomstick, and then back, it doesn't work for me."

"How was she killed?"

"Throat slit."

"That's up close and personal. Someone she knew, maybe."

"Gee, thanks, Sherlock."

"Signs of a struggle?"

"How 'bout we handle the investigation end of things for right now. If I need your help in that area, you'll be the first to know. Okay?"

"So, what do you want from me?"

The color seemed to drain from Manning's face. He actually looked pained, swallowed, and in almost a whisper, he said, "I could probably use your help, maybe."

A lesser man would have said no. Would have made him crawl, or stood up and walked out. I sat there staring into the paper cup at the baby-shit-brown latte, too shocked, too stunned to do anything. After a long moment, I looked up. "Are you fucking kidding me?"

"Look, you don't want to help and give this jerk a chance to slip away, there's nothing I can do about it. Not that I'm surprised. I thought you might want to help us out with something that can quickly turn into an ugly international incident here, but if—"

"I'll help," I said.

"You want to walk away that's—"

"I said I'll help, Manning. Stop beating me over the head and just tell me what you want me to do."

He studied me for a moment, his jaw sawing back and forth on his hapless piece of gum. The blue eyes were back to looking like lasers, and they zeroed in on me.

"Thanks, I appreciate it," he said, sounding a hundred percent genuine. "Here's what we're thinking. Someone fingered you, pardon the pun, tried to set you up. I'd like to play that card, make it look like you're our guy. See if that takes us anywhere."

"Okay," I said.

"Well, hang on, what this means is we may release your name to the media."

"Okay."

"Yeah, we'll play like we normally would. You're brought in for questioning as a suspect."

"I know how that part works," I said.

Manning gave me a genuine smile.

"We'll send you home, then pick you up tomorrow, make an arrest, and we'll release your name, say you're being held as a suspect."

"And?"

"And then we wait and see. We're looking at someone. We'll see if they make a move."

"Make a move?"

"Make a move," Manning said and didn't add anything.

"I'm glad to help, but I want my attorney in on this and Aaron LaZelle, too."

"LaZelle, your buddy over in vice?"

"Yeah, no offense, but if Louie and Aaron give the nod, I'm on board. It's not that I don't trust you, but I really have to be sure, okay?" I extended my hand over the desk.

"Not a problem. Under the circumstances, I'd do the same thing," he said and then shook my hand. "Haskell, for the record . . . thanks."

"For the record, Manning, if anyone can pull this off, you can. So get this bastard."

Thirty-two

ouie and Aaron gave their approval just before the noon hour in a conference room down the hall. Louie drew up the paperwork. Some guy named Captain Elkers, who Manning and most of the department seemed to report to, signed off on it, literally.

"Please don't take this the wrong way gentlemen, but my client, Mr. Haskell, has had a bit of a checkered history in some . . . shall we say, grey areas and I'd just like to be sure here. Once you sign this, absolving Mr. Haskell of any complacency, we can move ahead."

"Damn unorthodox," Captain Crabby grumbled but signed then quickly left the conference room.

Aaron looked serious but winked at me as he signed.

Manning signed and looked relieved.

"Thanks, Louie, I owe you dinner," I said.

"You'll owe me a lot more than that," he said. Then he looked over at Manning and asked, "What's the next step?"

"We release Mr. Haskell, and then we'll make a very public arrest later tomorrow, in time for the six o'clock news. Your choice where," Manning said, turning to me. "Home or the office."

"I think I'd prefer home. The office would be bad publicity."

Manning nodded. "You need a lift home."

"I can give you one," Louie said.

"Me too," Aaron said.

"Is Officer Trang available?"

"Yeah, I'll make sure she is," Manning said.

"Nothing personal, guys," I said.

"You're sure getting the special treatment," Officer Trang said. It was close to one-thirty by the time she was driving me home. As she spoke, she looked at me in her rearview mirror, viewing me through the heavy mesh screen.

"What can I say? I have that effect on folks."

"Gee, who knew? And all this while I was thinking that woman was right."

"Woman?" I asked.

"Menace and detriment are two of the words that spring to mind. I'm sure she has plenty of others."

"I'm sure she does. So, who did you piss off to get the short straw and draw this gig?"

"Driving you around?"

"Yeah."

"I was involved in an incident . . . standard procedure. You're off the street for a few days."

"Here I was thinking you were trying to get on Manning's good side."

"That would suggest he has one."

"You got me there. An incident . . . it wasn't that shooting? The one over on the Eastside, two or three nights ago?"

"Yeah," she answered, but with a tone that suggested she didn't care to go any further.

"Sorry, been there. So, you got time for a late lunch?"

Her eyes flashed in the rearview mirror, but I could detect a smile.

"Thanks, but no. How 'bout a rain check after hours sometime?"

"For sure, I've got a busy next few days, but maybe if you gave me your number."

She had just pulled to a stop in front of my house. Amazingly, the old bat with the little dog wasn't in sight to tell everyone what a low life I was. She didn't tell me her number, but climbed out, then opened the rear door for me.

"Here's my card," she said, smiling as she handed it to me. "Give me a call when things lighten up. I'd like that."

"You can count on it. Thanks, a real pleasure meeting you," I said, then held out my hand.

She took it, gave me a double squeeze, and maybe just the hint of a lingering look. Then she climbed back behind the wheel and drove off.

I felt my heart thumping, then slowly calming down as she turned at the corner. Now all I had to do was wait around until I got arrested.

It was a little after four the following afternoon. I'd just taken a couple of burritos out of the microwave, popped open a can of Dr. Pepper, and strolled into the living room to turn on the television. I glanced out the front window and noticed a Channel Four News van up the street with a black and white parked behind it. I looked down the street in the opposite direction. A black and white was parked on the far corner. I guessed there would be one or two uniforms in my back yard shortly if they weren't there already. They had really set the stage. I quickly gulped down my burrito, drank some of the Dr. Pepper, and thought I better use the bathroom, and put on a clean shirt for the cameras before they walked over and knocked on the door.

I was coming down the stairs maybe three minutes later. I thought I heard someone on the front porch and hoped it was luscious Officer Trang returning to put me in handcuffs.

I had one of those nanosecond thoughts. The police would ring the doorbell. I'd answer, "Hi guys, be with you in a minute let me just turn off the television and the kitchen lights. Anyone want a Dr. Pepper?"

That wasn't exactly how it went down. I was on the staircase, thought I heard shoes clomping, although in retrospect, they were wearing combat boots, not uniform shoes. As I descended the stairs, I could see trousers, Kevlar vests, shirt sleeves, protective plastic pads strapped over elbows and knees, all black. That should have been my first clue. St. Paul's finest usually wore blue uniforms. Clue number two would have been the locked door suddenly flying open and the six guys storming in with weapons drawn. Two guys flew into prone positions on my entryway rug and leveled automatic weapons at me. I didn't know what kind they were, AK's, maybe M-16s. All I saw was the wrong end of a couple hundred barrels, all pointing at me.

"Hands up, hands up!" someone screamed on the floor.

"Don't move, hands up!" another guy yelled from the doorway.

"Hey, watch the woodwork, damn it," I said and hurried down the steps, carrying my Dr. Pepper can to inspect my damaged doorframe.

"Don't move, hands up, get 'em up, get 'em up."

"Gun!" someone screamed.

I had about four steps left to descend, figuring I'd just calm everyone down when suddenly a very large arm grabbed my shirt, flung me over the railing, and slammed me onto the oak floor.

"Ughhh," was about all I got out as the wind was knocked out of me. Knees and feet pinned me to the floor, and someone seemed to be standing on my head.

"Freeze, asshole, don't move," someone yelled.

Move? That was the least of my problems. I couldn't breathe. I was struggling for air, panicking. Some guy was sitting on my chest, and I felt like it was collapsing. I couldn't move, couldn't get the weight off. I still couldn't breathe, more panic.

"Hold still, damn it," someone screamed as a pair of hands reached on either side of the boot standing on my skull and twisted my head, grinding my face into the floor. My nose gave an audible snap when it met the quarter-sawn oak floor, cutting off my air intake. I panicked even more and began to frantically struggle for air.

"Hold still, damn it." Someone slammed a boot or a fist a couple of times into my ribs just as my arms were twisted up behind my back, almost pulling them out of the sockets.

I vomited burrito and Dr. Pepper from the blows, coughed, and then gasped for more air.

"Oh, shit," a guy yelled, and the upper pressure on my right arm was relaxed.

From somewhere behind me on the stairs, another guy laughed.

I was too busy passing out to find anything funny.

When I regained consciousness, I was on my knees, vaguely aware my hands were cuffed behind my back. My head was held down, but not too forcefully. I could feel something cold moving back and forth across the back of my head.

"Just stay still, take some deep breaths, relax."

Yeah, I thought, that's what I'll do, relax. Footsteps were pounding up and down the staircase behind me. There were two or three pairs of black boots moving in and out of my peripheral vision. On the floor in front of me, blood continued to drip from my nose, forming a small pool. The nose wasn't working at the moment, and

I had to breathe through my mouth. The left sides of my upper and lower lip were swollen and torn, and my lower jaw was not quite lining up.

"Three pistols so far," a voice said. I heard the weapons bounce off one another, along with some rattling or crinkling. I guessed each weapon had been placed in a plastic evidence bag and was being handed to someone.

I attempted to say 'I'm licensed to carry,' but it came out as unintelligible garble.

"No one's talking to you, piece of shit. He good enough to travel?" A voice from somewhere above me thundered.

There must have been a response indicated.

"Good, then get him out of my sight. Nesbitt's out front with the brass doing the PR gig. Stuff him in a squad and take him downtown. They're waiting for him."

I was helped to my feet, pulled up by the shoulders by the two large cops dressed in black on either side of me. Lifting me up must have seemed like nothing more than throwing a beach ball around to the two of them. The guy on my left squeezed a blue gel pack in his hand. I half caught his eye as I stood.

"Thanks," I mumbled.

He looked at me with cold eyes, dropping the pack on the floor. "Shut the fuck up, asshole."

"Just a minute." A very large cop with a thick mustache, and a sinister-looking automatic weapon over his shoulder held his hand up. I thought he was the one who had asked if I could travel. He held the evidence bags with my pistols. For the first time, I saw SWAT in white letters across someone's back.

"Devlin Haskell, you have the right to remain silent…"

Eventually, I was led out the door toward a squad car waiting in my driveway with the lights flashing. There were two uniformed officers standing on the city sidewalk, talking to three different camera crews. My guess was it was the guy named Nesbitt, and some higher up puke that fascist with the mustache had mentioned.

The news crews rushed past him as soon as they saw me on the porch. A couple of uniforms made a half-hearted attempt to hold them back.

"Why did you kill Fiona Simmons?" a woman said into her microphone then thrust the thing in my direction. The microphone was fuzzy, grey, and looked like a Muppet on a stick. She looked familiar, the woman, but I couldn't place her.

"Where did you get the fingers?" some guy shouted. His toupee went slightly askew when he tried to duck under the arm of a police officer, and he quickly took a step back, indicating with a wave of his arm that the cameraman should focus on me being placed in the back of the squad car.

"Why were you stalking the English woman, Fiona Simmons?" another guy asked.

Cameras and news people clustered alongside the squad car as the two officers took their sweet time climbing in. We sat in my driveway for a good couple of minutes so everyone could get their shots of me arrested, handcuffed, and bloodied being taken downtown. A couple more camera flashes, and my post-traumatic stress was going to kick in.

As we backed out of the driveway, the woman with the fuzzy grey microphone was back on the sidewalk, pushing her microphone into the face of the old bat with the little white dog. She raised her hand, holding yet another bag of dog shit, and pointed at me as we drove away.

Thirty-three

We drove a different, less direct route than the one we took to the police station yesterday. But then, this entire experience had been a world of difference from my encounter with the beautiful Officer Trang.

"God, really sorry about that," the officer in the passenger seat said. He nodded in the direction of my head. I still couldn't breathe through my nose, and I was aware of the blood running over my lips, dripping onto my shirt. My left cheekbone felt like someone had taken a belt sander to it.

I half coughed and spit a mouthful of blood and mucus into the corner of the car floor in an attempt to clear my throat. The cop in the passenger seat turned around and glared at me for a second, then half smiled, looking friendly.

"Sometimes those SWAT guys get carried away, you know? Things just get out of hand even when it's a nice guy like you," the driver said. He looked at me in the rearview mirror, grey, lifeless eyes. I preferred the sparkles in Officer Trang's dark brown eyes from yesterday.

"Yeah, we'll get you checked out, make sure everything is okay. I'm wondering, Donny, if we shouldn't report this…Mr. Haskell being abused like this. It's just not right," passenger seat said.

Donny, the driver, nodded his agreement.

Passenger seat turned to face me again. "Any consolation, it probably feels and looks a lot worse than it actually is. You're young, day or two, hell you'll be good as new."

"Some folks just don't get it. It's like those skating chicks, the roller derby girls. They can say and do anything they please. Wear those outfits leaving nothing to the imagination. You and me make a comment, look at 'em wrong, next thing you know suddenly we're in trouble. What the hell is that all about?"

There it was my new pals. They were just letting me know they understood why I murdered Harlotte Davidson. Matter of fact might be a good idea to just get the whole thing off my chest, imagine how good I'd feel once I confessed and told them all about it.

I just stared out the window. We were going in the opposite direction from the police station, heading out Rice Street to Maryland Avenue, hopefully. With any luck, we'd cross over the freeway. The route just about tripled the time it took to get to the station. That left just enough time for me to confide the horrors of my crime to my two new best friends.

"You gotta wonder about some chick with the name Harlotte Davidson." Passenger seat leisurely chatted with Donny and me, trying a little different tack. "I mean, Harley builds the iconic American bike brand, and these English chicks, with no sense, go out and try to ruin the thing or ride on the coattails of all of Harley's hard work. What the hell is that about?" he asked, looking back at me.

Donny nodded his agreement.

I continued to look out the window. The Foundry bar was off on the left-hand side. We were crossing over 35E and heading up the Maryland Avenue hill. I picked up a girl at the Foundry one night a couple of years ago, or did she pick me up? I couldn't recall. Traci, Toni, Tina, I tried to recall her name. I remembered she'd had a lacy tattoo on her lower back, running from hip to hip. Red roses, with little stars and a banner in the center across a large heart that read *'Pleased to Meet You.'*

I just concentrated on trying to remember her name and hoped these two delivered me into Manning's protective custody sooner rather than later.

"Not only that," Donny said. He was turning onto Payne Avenue, heading back toward the station, ten minutes tops, I guessed. "What does that do to the sense of morality in the country? Like it isn't tough enough teaching kids the lessons of our Lord and Savior Jesus Christ." Passenger seat gave him a look that suggested they'd most likely reached the end of their probing routine.

Tally, Teresa, Twyla, I concentrated, kept trying to come up with her name. She had black hair a little more than shoulder length, black hair with white blonde high-lights. She had a little diamond pierced on the left side of her nose. She'd had a belly button ring with a large blue stone. My head was throbbing.

"You follow that roller derby much?" Donny asked. It was his last shot. We were pulling up in front of the building, parking almost exactly where the luscious Officer Trang had pulled in just yesterday. His voice sounded hopeful, but his eyes reflected the same lifeless grey in the rearview mirror.

"Give it a rest, Donny," passenger seat said. "They're waiting for you up in interview room one, ass-hole." Then he groaned as he climbed out and stepped over to open the rear door for me.

Interview room one. At least I'd be in familiar sur-roundings.

"Tonya," I said, as he helped me out.

"What?"

"Tonya, the girl at the Foundry, with the blonde highlights in her hair, '*Pleased to Meet You*' tattooed on her lower back."

Thirty-four

I hadn't been seated at the table in the interview room for more than a couple of minutes before the door opened, and Louie came bouncing in. Manning was right behind him.

"So, how'd it go public enemy number—" Louie's eyes went wide as he looked at me beaten up, bloody and bruised. He rushed over to me, tossing his briefcase onto the floor.

"Been better," I gurgled, then coughed up some more blood.

"What the—" Louie started to say.

"Jesus Christ, what the hell happened?" Manning asked. He hadn't moved more than a couple of feet into the room and sounded genuinely concerned.

Louie turned on him and exploded. "This is your idea of cooperation? You beat the shit out of the guy. What the hell is wrong with you idiots? The deal is off, right now, we're finished. Tell your people to get ready for a brutality suit. This is—"

Manning had already picked up the wall phone and waved Louie quiet.

"Interview room one, now, we need medical assistance. Now, goddamnit! And find Elkers. I want him in here." He shook his head as he listened to a response, all the while saying, "No, no, no," in a low voice. All of a sudden, he erupted into the phone. "I don't care who in the hell he's meeting with, you tell him interview room one, now," he screamed and slammed the receiver back into place. He took a deep breath and turned to face us.

I attempted to shrug and smile, but it hurt so much I stopped halfway through.

"Jesus, you attempt to resist arrest?" Manning smiled, but his heart wasn't in the joke, and his head was quickly growing from scarlet to purple.

"We are so fucking through with this agreement to cooperate, and you are going to have one hell of a lawsuit on—"

"Look, I have no idea what happened. We were supposed to send a squad to bring you in, some news cameras. What the hell happened?"

I gave another half-hearted shrug and grimaced for added effect.

"Give me a couple of minutes to find—"

There was a knock on the door, and two EMTs hurried in wheeling a stretcher, with a black medical bag sitting on top of it. They wore navy blue trousers and short-sleeved white shirts with a red fire department patch on the shoulder. They were pulling surgical gloves on as they entered.

Manning jerked his scarlet head in my direction.

Louie took a step back as they approached, patted me on the shoulder, and said, "Hang in there, buddy." Then, he motioned Manning to a distant corner of the interview room.

The EMTs started in with a blood pressure cuff and a penlight shining in my eyes. With them hovering over me and asking questions, I couldn't see or hear exactly what was said between Louie and Manning, but most of it seemed to be unpleasant and sounded like it was coming from Louie. There was just the occasional word or grunt of acquiescence from Manning.

The EMTs were applying creams to my cheekbone and then a bandage. "You're not going to need stitches. It's just a little raw." Once they cleaned up my face, they smeared some menthol salve on my lips that burned and reminded me of a bad curry dish I'd gotten sick on a while back.

"How many times has that nose been broken?" one of them asked as he knelt down in front of me. He was a red-headed guy, average size, lots of freckles, soft voice.

"More than twice," I said and then coughed more blood.

"I'm gonna reset it. If that's okay, it will help clear up those air passages. That all right with you?"

"Go for it, Doc," I said, then grabbed onto the side of the table for support.

He placed his hands on either side of my nose and gave a brief look at his partner, who opened the medical bag and slowly pulled something out.

I glanced down to see what the partner was getting, felt a sudden pressure, and heard an audible snap.

"Ouch, Jesus," I half screamed.

Manning and Louie looked over in our direction.

"There," he said." Back to a thing of beauty. You'll live, but you probably know the drill…swelling for a few days, eyes will blacken. This will help open that up," he said. Then pulled out a reddish rubber ball thing with a small pointed end. It looked like a miniature turkey baster. He gently inserted it into my nasal passage.

"Just aspirating here, get some of that blood and mucus out. Believe me, this will be a lot better than trying to blow it out later tonight."

The door opened, and Captain Elkers stepped in. He took one look at me, saw the conference in the corner, and headed toward Manning. Before the door had closed completely, Aaron LaZelle pushed the door open and entered the room.

Aaron took one look at me, mouthed the word 'Jesus,' and joined the conference heating up in the corner.

I winced as one of the EMTs placed some pressure on my ribs.

"Oh, what's this?" he said, lifting a stethoscope from around his neck.

"Someone tried to get my attention." I grimaced and exhaled.

"Let me just lift that shirt. Mmm-mmm," he said, looking over my rib cage. "Anything here?" he asked, pressing up and down my left side.

"No, nothing."

"And here?" he said, doing the same on my right, but a lot more gently.

"Yeah, oh Jesus, yeah, that hurts."

He was on it with the stethoscope, gently, listening to my breathing.

"I want you to raise your arms to shoulder height, take some deep breaths if you can. Okay?"

I nodded and did the deep breathing routine. It was sore, but not as bad as I'd feared. My guess was they weren't broken.

"I don't think they're broken, just a little bruised…nothing forty-eight hours and taking it easy won't help heal. You're a bit banged up, but you'll live. If you want, we can maybe transport you for x-rays."

"You recommend that?"

"Oh, I don't think it's necessary, but I suspect this might be on the city's nickel," he said under his breath, then gave a nod to the far corner where Manning was getting it from Louie, Aaron and Captain Elkers. I thought I might have detected the hint of a smile from the EMT. "I suppose if there's nothing else I could give them the word."

"Nah, I don't want to do x-rays. I think I'll be fine, but maybe we could let them discuss things a little longer," I said, then moved my head in the direction of the conference corner.

Louie was in the process of jabbing a finger at Captain Elkers, and I heard the words, "with your goddamned signature," and a little later, "grabbing headlines".

"Be fun to watch," The EMT smiled. "But if this is all we better get going, maybe take some extra-strength Tylenol for a couple of days to make you a little more comfortable."

"Thanks, no offense, but I hope I don't see you around, Doc."

He laughed and started placing things back into the medical bag. He tossed the bag on the stretcher, and while his partner wheeled it toward the door, he approached the group. Some low key murmurs followed, nodding, the occasional excitable outburst from Louie as the EMT continued to speak in low tones, and then he nodded and left, giving me a wink on the way out.

Louie strolled over, opened his briefcase, and spoke to me under his breath.

"Turn around and face me."

"What?"

"Turn toward me, I need a picture," he said, pulling a digital camera out of his briefcase.

I turned sideways in my chair. Louie quickly shifted a couple steps to the side. He was going to photograph me with Manning and Elkers in the background. Unfortunately, Aaron would be in the photo, too.

"Look toward the mirrors," he whispered. The flash went off before I heard the camera click.

"What the…oh shit," Elkers said.

Flash. Flash.

Elkers stormed past, red-faced.

"Nice chatting with you, Captain," I said as he tore open the door and fled the room.

Louie moved around me, taking more photos, talking to Manning as the camera flashed.

"We'll need a driver. My client, Mr. Haskell will not be remaining in custody. Under the circumstances, I just don't think your department is up to the task."

Flash.

Manning looked like he was going to kill, but I'm not sure he was thinking of Louie or me as his intended targets.

Flash.

"Lift the shirt up, Dev. Let's see those ribs."

I pulled my shirt up, slowly, maybe a little too dramatically.

"Oh my God," Louie said.

Flash.

"Christ, let me get some things arranged for you. You want anything?" Manning asked. He was standing with the door open, still red-faced, but at least not heading toward purple any longer.

Flash.

"No, I think you've all done more than enough already," Louie said, then took a couple more shots of my bruised ribs.

Manning nodded and left. Aaron walked over, waiting while Louie took a few more shots of my face from different angles.

"I don't know what it is with you people," Louie said.

"Hey, Louie, relax. He's a pal. And stop flashing that damn camera, you're driving me nuts," I said.

"Dev, what the hell happened? You were supposed to come nicely," Aaron said. "You hit on one of the arresting officers' wives in the recent past?"

"If I did, she most likely turned me down."

"So, what happened?"

"I don't know. Those SWAT guys just—"

"SWAT? They sent the SWAT team out there?"

"Yeah. I looked out the window, saw a couple of black and whites on the street, a television news van. I knew why they were there, so I went upstairs to get a clean shirt, pee…the next thing I know, they kicked in my front door."

"What?"

"Yeah, I was ready to let them in, coming down the stairs to open the door and ask 'em if they wanted something to drink."

"Did they pound on the door or anything when you were upstairs?"

"No, nothing, believe me. I thought it was going to be a nice guy, laid back deal. Next thing I know, the door gets kicked open, and I'm looking down the barrel of a couple of AK's. Then some guy grabs me and throws me over the banister. They weren't kidding around."

"Christ, that's Elkers. He must have lined that up, wanted to go for the action shot," Aaron said.

"Hey, you got an action shot, all right. We'll subpoena the news tapes," Louie said, then smiled coldly at Aaron.

"Dev, I'm truly sorry. It wasn't supposed to go down like this," Aaron said.

"You realize, Lieutenant, that—"

"Give it a rest, Louie," I said. "Where do we go from here?"

"Well, here's the deal, obviously this thing has turned into a cluster fuck. That said, there's no doubt it will be running on the news tonight. The arrest of a stalker and killer." He turned to look at Louie. "If you're going to pursue the police brutality angle, and of course you've got your signed agreement, it would seem to me running on tonight's news could only help your case," Aaron said.

I nodded, it made sense.

"Based on what you tell me, I agree with your attorney. You shouldn't stay in protective or segregated custody here. You can, however, get us to pick up the tab on a fairly luxurious stay at some hotel. Eat some good meals for a change, take a few days off, rest up. Hopefully, someone will surface once they believe we've got you locked up, and the coast is clear," Aaron said.

"And if they don't surface?" Louie asked.

"Sue our ass one way or the other. Under the circumstances, you hold all the cards. Like I said before, after today's incident, continued cooperation on your part would only seem to strengthen your chances with any lawsuit you decide to bring down the road."

Thirty-five

We were seated at a large polished table in my hotel suite. The curtains were drawn back, so we had a view of the boat traffic on the Mississippi as the sun set off to the west. The sunset was a gorgeous orange and reflected down the length of the river. A large white boat with a red paddlewheel had just begun heading upriver on its evening excursion.

I felt a lot better after the massage, a hot soak in the tub, and an hour nap. I sipped some more wine and cut another piece from the perfectly grilled steak on my plate. I adjusted the thick, white terrycloth robe and got just a little more comfortable. Then I clicked the remote to turn up the music and dim the lights over the table ever so slightly.

"More wine, my darling?" I asked.

"No, I better watch it. I gotta drive home," Louie said, then burped some steak and baked potato.

"Since when did you get so responsible? Come on."

"No, I better not. Tell you what, you got a cold Summit or a Leinenkugel behind the bar there, I'll take it."

"Help yourself. I'm the patient, remember? I'm supposed to take it easy."

"Man, Dev, you're lucky those guys didn't do some serious damage."

"They kicked in the door, splintered my damn door frame, all to hell, that's enough damage for me."

"You know what I mean," Louie said. "Good thing you bounce well. A classic case of the right hand not knowing what the left was doing."

"No Louie, classic case of someone going in to grab headlines, steal all the credit, and doesn't communicate with the guys in the trenches doing the heavy lifting. Elkers was floating around, knowing the press had been alerted. He moved things up a notch and got the SWAT team to barge in, instead of some baby faced rookie knocking on my door asking politely if I could accompany him downtown."

"But still, they should have taken it easy. No need for that rough shit," Louie said. He was down on his knees behind the marble-topped bar, rummaging around in the fridge. "Man, this place is well stocked," he said, standing up. He held a green bottle of some kind of German beer, opened it, and poured it into a chilled glass.

"The SWAT guys might have been jerks, but they didn't know it was all prearranged. Far as they knew I was a baddy who murdered a woman. They bagged my pistols. I don't like it, but you can't really blame them. I can, however, blame Elkers."

"Yeah, and there he was tonight on the news, standing in front of your place, taking questions from those reporters when they hauled you out, cuffed, beautiful, man. And then all those reporters while you're sitting in the back of the squad car with the shit kicked out of you." Louie waddled back to join me at the dining room table. "It's like your buddy Aaron said, the news footage can only help us."

"Now if they can just get the guy who did this. Think Manning will take much flak on this?"

"Manning? What do you care?"

"I sort of like the guy. He can be a pain in the ass, but he's a straight shooter. If nothing else, the guy is honest."

"No, I don't think he'll get much heat." Louie gulped down a healthy amount of beer. "He'll get some, but with all the news footage, it's too high profile. But I'll tell you. I wouldn't want to be Elkers tonight."

"What do you think will happen?"

"To Elkers?"

I nodded.

"He's history. It might be a resignation for the good of the department deal or just a quiet retirement six months down the road, but either way, I'd guess he's gone. Too bad, it's a tough way to go, with no one to blame but his own ego," Louie said, then gulped more beer.

"I just want them to get the guy who killed Fiona Simmons."

"Yeah," Louie said. He was up and making his way behind the bar, again. "We need to talk about what you want by way of damages. This all-expense paid visit to the hotel is nice, but you got all the cards, my friend, with a lot more available."

"Louie, I got kicked around a little. I'm not wild about it, but in a day or two, I should be pretty much back to normal."

"Yeah, whatever normal is, in your case." He was standing behind the marble-topped bar, watching the frost melt off the exterior of the fresh glass as he poured another beer.

"Think about this," he said. "You've got the physical beating, plus the damage to your reputation, repetitional damage to your business, physical damage to your home, and then there are all the psychological issues…"

"Psychological issues?"

"Believe me, Dev, you got 'em," he said, then drained a third of his glass and looked around. "Man, that is good. Hey, this joint got an extra bed?"

Thirty-six

I had the feeling the guy on the other end of the phone was doing a half dozen other things while answering my call. I could hear the general hum of conversations in the background.

"Detective Manning, please," I said.

"Who's calling?"

"Devlin Haskell," I said, not really sure I should be giving him my name.

"Just a moment, Sir." He had sort of snapped to, or was I just imagining? Didn't matter, Manning was always good for a ten-minute wait before he bothered to pick up the phone.

I'd just finished the order of Eggs Benedict plus the side plate of smoked salmon and caviar that room service had delivered. I poured another cup of coffee and glanced at my watch. Nine-fifty in the morning. Louie had left an hour earlier. I had another massage and a spa treatment scheduled for eleven. That left enough time for at least two more of those really tasty blueberry muffins.

"This is Detective Manning."

I checked my watch. It was still nine-fifty.

"Detective Manning, Dev Haskell. Didn't expect you to pick up so fast."

"How's it going?" he asked, actually sounding genuine.

"I've got two of the most gorgeous black eyes you've ever seen."

"How are you feeling?" he said, quickly moving on from my black eyes.

"I'll live. Anything turn up yet?"

"You mean like a suspect with a note pinned to his coat that says I'm guilty?"

"Could it be that easy?" I asked.

"No, we're more or less in the wait-and-see mode over here, shining a little light under the occasional rock."

Not the answer I was hoping for.

"Anything I can do to help?" I asked.

"Yeah, continue to keep a low profile, rest up, take it easy in that hotel suite. How's the food?"

We chatted on for a minute or two about my Eggs Benedict and then absolutely nothing important. I had the feeling the guy was really trying, but then another look in the bathroom mirror at my two black eyes, my nose, and my banged-up face made me think he should.

It was during my late morning massage that I got to thinking about what I could do to help catch Fiona's murderer. The guy obviously was aware of the Hastings Hustlers' schedule, the various cities where they were appearing. That narrowed the field down to anyone in the world with Internet access.

I drifted back to the two cops who transported me yesterday. They tried the anti-woman angle, the religious angle, and the stalker angle. Was it one of those? The guy had clearly been stalking Fiona, but why? A perceived slight? Maybe some flake who followed her over here from England? Some Jodie Foster type of stalker?

The only cameras at the hotel where Fiona was murdered were the ones carried by the guests. Late-night hotel security consisted of a fifty-something woman with a bourbon buzz at the front desk and the pool maintenance guy. Fiona had been found in her room with her throat slit. The stalker seemed to know what hotels the team was going to be staying in. In fact, in the case of Chicago and St. Paul, he knew the actual room she was in. Twice in St. Paul, now that I thought about it, once to firebomb her and then, well, the second incident, her murder.

I felt the masseuse kneading my back. He moved cautiously around the ribs on my right side and seemed to know what he was doing. I was completely relaxed. He had just massaged some hot, fragrant oil into my back and was in the process of laying smooth, hot stones along my spine and shoulders. I had to admit, this was the life. Things were really going well if you glossed over my beating. I figured I could milk this luxury hotel stay for at least a good week. But there was a dark cloud if my past history served as any kind of lesson, this was exactly the time when I usually screwed things up.

Thirty-seven

No one was around when the taxi dropped me off down the block behind my parked car. I could see a white carpenter's van parked in my drive-way, saw horses supporting a number of different boards. Tools were set up across my front lawn, and there was a guy hammering around my front door frame. I decided nothing positive could come from poking my nose in, plus I wasn't supposed to be here, so I climbed in my car and drove off. No point in alerting Manning that I had wandered off the luxury reservation.

I was thinking about the fingers as I drove. They'd been frozen, which maybe made sense. Did some guy have a bucket of them in a freezer, and he grabbed one whenever needed, a little different version of giving someone the finger? That seemed to make a lot more sense than some guy cutting off a fresh finger every time the Hastings Hustlers appeared in a new town. But then why would he leave one of the things in my garage?

I ended up in the library, doing what I should have done a long time ago. I Googled the Hastings Hustlers. From all the searching I did, which was only an hour on the library computer before my time was up, I couldn't find any mention of fingers sent to anyone on the team. For that matter, I couldn't find mention of fingers sent to anyone, anywhere, until the Hustlers arrived in the United States.

There were, however, three separate incidents back in the UK of property damage to some of the Hustlers' cars while the team practiced at night. One was spray painted, another had a windshield broken, and a third had all four tires slit. All this occurred in the two months before they flew over for their fundraising tour.

I drove back to the hotel to soak in my Jacuzzi and gave Manning a call. The Jacuzzi was an octagonal affair that would easily fit a half dozen people. It sat in a mirrored room off the bathroom so no matter which direction I looked, I could see myself through the steamed-up mirrors. The phone was mounted on the wall behind me, and I had the Jacuzzi jets rumbling, causing the bubble bath to form a mountain of suds.

"Who's calling?" I thought it was the same guy who'd answered the phone earlier in the morning, but I couldn't be sure. It still sounded like he was doing a number of different things while he answered my call.

"Dev Haskell." I expected to get a sense of him straightening up when he heard my name.

"Let me see if I can find him," he said, then dropped the receiver on the desk or maybe the floor. The bang caused me to jump. Things must have been getting back to normal because Manning didn't pick up for a good five minutes. I almost dozed off.

"Detective Manning."

"Dev Haskell," I said, then waited, a very long moment before I followed with," I was doing some research, on the computer."

"And?" Manning said. I had the feeling he may have counted to ten before speaking.

"And, I found at least three incidents of damage to vehicles belonging to members of the Hustlers team back in the UK. Before they came to the states."

"Okay," Manning said, then sounded like he was whispering to someone else.

I waited for a further response, but one didn't seem to be coming.

"Well, I thought it might be of interest. Someone or some group, vandalizing their vehicles before they came over to the US…the first incident was almost two months before they arrived here.

"Yeah, that was the spray paint, right?"

"Yeah, and then the windshield about three weeks . . . oh, so you're aware of all this?"

"Yeah, Sherlock. The last incident, someone slit her tires, all four of them. Maybe about a week before they came over."

"Her tires?"

"What?"

"You said her tires. All three of these incidents targeted Fiona's car."

"Yeah. Of course, it's hard to miss a red Mercedes S400, but you didn't hear that from me. And why aren't you busy watching soft porn in your penthouse suite or lurking around the hotel lobby annoying female guests instead of wasting my time with yesterday's news? Where the hell are you, anyway?"

"I'm at the hotel."

"Sounds like you're riding in the back of a truck. What the hell is that noise?" he asked.

"I think they're vacuuming out in the hall," I said, then turned down the Jacuzzi jets. "It would have been nice to know about the vandalism to her car. Three separate incidents? Think it's the same guy? An S400…that's kind of pricy, don't you think?"

"If you have to ask, you can't afford. The things go for about ninety grand and up. But, last time I checked, you weren't a part of this official investigation. Look, Haskell, don't take this wrong. I'm genuinely sorry about the dumb headed jackass incident yesterday. Honest, I really am. You didn't, well in fact, no one deserves that. And I'm sure we haven't heard the last of it. Now, I appreciate your attempt to help. That said, there is still an official, ongoing investigation into the death of Fiona Simmons, and unless I'm told differently, you're not involved."

"Anything on the DNA results from the fingers?"

"Like I said, you're not involved, Mr. Haskell. Now, I should probably get back to work and see if I can accomplish something today, and you can spend more of the city's money in that luxury suite if there's nothing else."

"No, I guess that's about it, Detective."

"Good. Hey, I appreciate your concern, soon as we have something confirmed, we'll alert the media. You can learn about it that way. Thank you," he said and hung up.

I had a vision of Manning standing in his cubicle once he hung up, head going scarlet and screaming at everyone within earshot. "From now on, no one is to answer my stupid phone calls."

He did set me straight on one thing. If it was the same guy in the UK and over here whoever he was, he hadn't been targeting the Hustlers. He'd been going after Fiona right from the start. And the car, a Mercedes S400? If only I could figure out why?

Thirty-eight

Who knew you could order a laptop from room service? Thank God for Manning's advice to spend the city's money. I felt like a movie star. I had pushed aside the dishes from my steak dinner and was working my way through an ice bucket crammed with chilled bottles of Summit Extra Pale. It was a little after midnight. The curtains were still pulled back on the windows, and outside the moon reflected off the surface of the river. An occasional car's headlights slowly illuminated the downtown bridges as they worked its way over the river. The city appeared to be asleep.

I'd been reading online about the Hastings Hustlers beginning with their inception forty-three years earlier. Fiona Simmons had been just the latest legend. Their fundraising success seemed to always revolve around one major superstar. Fiona had been the most recent. Did that suggest a jealous boyfriend or husband? Maybe, although her husband had been in the UK watching their kids the entire time. Pretty tough to tape a finger to a bus door in Denver or shove it under the hotel room door in Chicago from that distance.

Did she have a boyfriend? Maybe, but from my brief dealings with her, it seemed unlikely. After all, she hadn't made a pass at me. Just kidding.

The team website posted a roster. I made a note to myself to place some phone calls to the girls in the morning. I shut down my new computer, clicked the porn channel on with the remote, and promptly fell asleep.

"You see the news this morning?" Louie asked once I picked up the phone. It was just after ten and a gorgeous sunny day. The river sparkled like someone had sprinkled gold glitter up and down the channel as far as the eye could see. Small boats raced back and forth, passing under the downtown bridges, no doubt heading to beaches or favorite fishing holes.

I was wrapped in the hotel's white terrycloth bathrobe, just finishing my order of Eggs Benedict. The phone was wedged between my ear and shoulder as I stuffed the last corner of English muffin, ham and hollandaise sauce into my mouth, then scooped up more hollandaise and licked the fork.

"They're having that big memorial bout for Fiona Simmons tonight, at the Veteran's Auditorium," he said.

"Really? I better get off the phone. I'm sure they're trying to call me right now to help with their security concerns."

"Yeah, well, don't hold your breath. Besides, as far as they know, you're under lock and key in the darkest, blackest hole in jail."

"Oh, yeah, that."

"You are staying put, right? Please tell me you're not going out and doing anything crazy."

"Me? No. I'm staying here. I got a massage scheduled for one, probably a nap after that, room service, that's as wild as I plan to be."

"Nice work if you can get it."

"Yeah, well, I don't recommend the route I took to get here."

"Oh, this doesn't even begin to count on what you're going to get. I went ahead and subpoenaed the news footage. That old broad, holding the bag of dog shit will play beautifully in the defamation suit."

"She'd slit her wrists if she knew she'd done me a favor."

I hung up with Louie and then called down to the front desk.

"Hi, this is Dev Haskell, up in the penthouse suite."

"Yes, sir, what may I do for you?" a friendly female voice asked.

"I wonder if I can have you order some tickets for me. Just bill it to my room, and I can settle up when I check out?"

"Not a problem, I'd be happy to help, sir. We do add a five percent service charge, sir."

"That's fine."

"Were you thinking of anything in particular? If I might suggest some of the standard popular items, the Guthrie Theatre is presenting an interpretation of Shakespeare's Macbeth. The Xcel Center is hosting Lionel

Richie. I'm not sure on availability there, but we can try. Norah Jones is at the Ordway. I think that's sold out. The Twins are playing Kansas City tonight . . ."

She seemed to be reading off a screen, and I figured she would be able to go on for a lot longer than I cared to listen.

"Actually, great as all that sounds, I wanted to get a couple of tickets to the Memorial roller derby bout tonight over at Veteran's Auditorium."

"Oh, between the Bombshells and that English team, The Hastings Hustlers. Great choice, it's a hot ticket. I'm checking now. Bear with me while I get that site up on my screen here and see."

Either she was the consummate professional, or I was out of the roller derby demographic. I was half surprised I could even order tickets online.

"Sorry, sir, it's taking a little longer than . . . oh, here we go. Okay, ticket availability, let's see. Oh, looks to be pretty much sold out. There are a few tickets left. They're actually in the private boxes. I've got four at one-fifty each. They're on the end, two sets of two for one-seventy-five each, both boxes on the side."

"Those will do, two for one-seventy-five each."

"I've two locations, sir. One is—"

"You choose one, and that will be fine. Do I pick those tickets up at the front desk tonight?"

"Actually, no, sir. They'll be waiting for you at the ticket window at the Veteran's Auditorium. You'll need to have a photo ID when you pick them up. They'll be waiting for you under your name, Devlin Haskell," she said, then followed up by spelling my last name.

"Great."

"Anything else I can help you with, sir?"

"No, thanks, you've been very helpful."

I hung up and made another call. She answered on the fourth ring.

"Hello."

"Hi, Heidi, Dev."

"Oh Dev, what did you do?"

"What?"

"What do you mean, what? I watch the news from time to time. I saw your arrest on the news. Look, thanks for the memories, but I'm not posting bail this time. I'm really sorry, but I don't want to be involved."

"Okay. Listen, you busy tonight?"

"What?"

"I asked, are you busy tonight? Do you want to go out?"

"With you?"

"No, some other guy I'm fixing you up with. Yes, with me."

"But your arrest? It was on the news."

"Actually, that's a long story. Join me for dinner?"

"Um, well, yeah. Yeah, I suppose. Okay. You're sure? Where are you, by the way? I thought you—"

"Yeah. Look, I'll explain everything over dinner. Beef Bourguignon, okay with you?"

"You know I love it. Um, yeah, I guess. Just a little surprising is all. Where are you?"

"I'm downtown in the penthouse . . . " The bout started at eight, Heidi was going to join me in my suite at six for dinner. I phoned room service and ordered dinner with a couple of bottles of wine, and then left for my spa appointment.

After my massage and a brief nap, I phoned the Hustlers hotel and worked my way through the team roster posing as a reporter. I had a vague recollection of having been introduced to some of the names, but could only conjure up a rough image on three of the girls. An hour and a half later, I knew a little more, but not much.

I'd gotten an inkling of some pretty heavy-duty fundraising and the distinct possibility that superstar, Fiona Simmons, AKA Harlotte Davidson, had been receiving a contractual percentage. That could explain the Mercedes, maybe.

Thirty-nine

Room service rolled in a bucket of chilled white wine at precisely five-fifty that evening. I spent the next twenty minutes looking out the window, watching the traffic fifteen stories below to see if I could spot Heidi's BMW. She arrived a stylish half-hour late at six-thirty.

"God, check this place out," she said, walking into my suite, wide eyed. She ran over to the wall of windows to look out. She was wearing a skirt, the length of some of my belts. It would never allow her to even think about sitting modestly. She had on a low cut top displaying her Grand Canyon of cleavage with a little gold crucifix hanging around her neck. Who could blame the man for staring down into the abyss?

"Hi, Heidi, I'm fine. Thanks for asking."

"This place is fantastic. The view, oh my God," she said, stretching to look upriver. What there was of her skirt skidded up over her perfect rear. Eventually, I noticed that the heels she had on sported wedges on the soles about an inch thick, which allowed the heels to be even higher.

"Care for a glass of wine?" I shook myself back to the moment.

"Okay, fess up. What's going on? The news had you down as a local Charles Manson," she said, turning away from the window. By the way, what's up with the black eyes?"

"Police brutality," I said, then swept my arm around in a grand gesture to encompass the suite.

"Huh?"

I poured some white wine and went on to explain about Justine, the Hustlers, the police surveillance on me, Fiona's murder, the signed agreement, and the SWAT team. There was the possibility I left some things out. Cut off fingers come to mind, and I may have colored some other areas a bit in my favor.

"Wow, you've been busy. How do you always end up in these situations?" she asked, and then sipped.

"I'm not sure. It just seems to happen, I guess."

"Let me get this straight. You start out helping some woman you met in a bar and end up handcuffed and a murder suspect? That's not normal."

"What can I say?"

"Maybe nothing would be best."

There was a knock on the door— room service with our dinner. The room service guy set out our table, smiled, poured red wine into crystal glasses, set out the salad plates, poured the dressing, positioned the bread-basket, then dished up our plates from two silver trays, one holding the beef bourguignon and another baked potatoes. I had purposely requested no vegetable. Then he lingered around, making busy and leering at Heidi's ass. I handed him a five, which he quickly pocketed, gave Heidi a final glance, and scooted for the door.

"Thank you," I called, closing the door behind him. He was already halfway down the hall.

"Dinner, Heidi?" I said, pulling a chair out for her.

"You sure I'm not going to get stuck with the bill here?" she said as she sat down.

"Jesus, when did we become so cynical?"

"No offense, but it's become a habit when you're involved. Just remember, I'm usually your first call for bail money. Remember that insurance deal? Then the time you hid out at my place. There was that night you—"

"Okay, give it a rest. I thought you'd enjoy a nice dinner and a fun night out. If it's going to be a problem, never mind. We can skip the meal and just hop in the sack and get to it."

"Dinner will be fine, thank you."

We had finished eating and were working our way through the second bottle of wine, a Chateaneuf du Pape, which I had only heard of, and Heidi had declared "absolutely divine."

I came out of the bathroom and took another sip of wine. Heidi was back at the window, watching the river traffic.

"Okay, finish that up. We gotta get going here," I said.

"Get going? Where?"

"I have box tickets lined up for tonight's entertainment," I said.

"You're kidding."

"No, I'm not kidding. What's with all this negativity? I ask you out for a nice meal, an evening's entertainment and you want to question everything. We can skip the show if you want."

"Sorry, guess I'm just not used to it. Let me run to the little girl's room for a minute, and I'll be right back."

I'd waited for Heidi before on her runs to little girl's rooms. I topped up my wine glass, walked over to the windows and watched the beginning of a gorgeous sunset, counted the boats on the river, stared at the evening traffic, watched some folks picnicking in the park across the river.

"Okay, all set," she said, coming out of the bathroom.

I'd set my empty glass on the table five minutes earlier.

"You're sure there's nothing else you have to do? A Jacuzzi, make up, brush your hair?"

"Does my hair look okay?" She was serious.

"Come on, let's go."

Forty

It was a gorgeous evening. The hotel was only three blocks from the Veteran's Auditorium, and so we decided to walk. Besides, Heidi wouldn't have been caught dead in my car under any circumstances.

The auditorium stood next to the Xcel Center, where Lionel Richie was appearing. In fact, the auditorium entrance actually looked like a side entrance to the Xcel Center. We were still maybe a half block away, Heidi had hung onto my arm and chatted the entire two and a half blocks. Four or five glasses of wine did that to her. She was taking tiny steps in those shoes with the skyscraper stiletto heels about ten inches high and seemed oblivious to the constantly turning heads and the car horns honking at her.

"Oh, God, Lionel Richie. I just adore him," she said, looking at the lighted marquee hanging above the grand entrance to the Xcel Center. It flashed two messages, '*Lionel Richie*' in big swirling letters hung there for about ten seconds. Then, it faded dark before '*Appearing Tonight Only*' came on, and in a slightly smaller, bold type '*Sold Out*' flashed three or four times.

"Well, actually . . ."

She squeezed my arm tighter, then reached up and planted a kiss on my cheek. What there was of her skirt rose up again over that perfect ass. A passing car slowed and honked at her a couple of times as a thank you. "God, I tried to get tickets, but he was sold out before I was even able to log on. You are so sweet, Dev."

"Let's just slip in this side entrance and avoid the crowds," I said, passing beneath the industrial street sign that identified the Veteran's Auditorium entrance.

Once inside, we found ourselves on a concourse that seemed to be inhabited by two completely different groups of people. There was a forty-plus, chilled white wine type of crowd, couples in slacks or skirts, hair done, diamonds, pearls, all heading up the concourse into the Xcel Center. Or the designer jean, Jell-o shots and T-shirt crowd heading down into the Veteran's Auditorium, we followed downstream.

"You sure we're going the right way?" She took a quick glance over her shoulder as we moved away from Lionel Richie's fans, but she had to turn around to keep her balance in her heels.

"We have to go this way to get into our private box," I said.

"A private box? I am *so* going to ride you, Mister," Heidi said. Her eyes brightened, and she hung even tighter on my arm, rubbing against me as we walked.

The jig was up when we stopped at the ticket window.

"I'll need a picture I.D. please."

"Devlin Haskell, two tickets. It's for a private box, actually," I said to the young Goth-looking woman on the other side of the counter, then flashed my driver's license.

Heidi continued to hang onto my arm but leaned back to read the 'Veteran's Auditorium Tickets' sign above the window.

"Private box for the Bombshells and Hastings Hustlers, right." The woman nodded. She had what looked like the better part of a car grill pierced through her left eyebrow and along the upper ridge of both ears.

"What? There better be a lot to drink in that private box," Heidi said, then pinched my arm, hard.

We rode up two escalators, which gave a lot of roller derby enthusiasts a chance to be enthusiastic about Heidi's dress or the lack of it. She was too busy looking at tattoos and cursing me to notice or care.

Our private box was midway down a corridor and attended by a nice little redheaded girl who looked all of twelve. She had tattoos covering both her arms from the wrists up to and beyond the short sleeves on her white blouse. She opened the door and stepped aside so we could walk in.

"If there's anything you guys need, just let me know. I'm Destiny," she said.

"I'll start with a vodka martini, better make it a double," Heidi said.

"Actually, there's like a totally full bar, blender, ice, mix, beer, and really cool snacks in the box. You can just help yourself." Destiny smiled.

"Good," Heidi said and strutted past me to familiarize herself with the bar.

"We've got your credit information, so we just charge your card for whatever you use." Destiny continued to smile.

"Thanks, I'm sure we'll be fine," I said, then took a deep breath and turned to face Heidi as Destiny closed the door and left me to fate.

Forty-one

The private box had two rows of tier seating made up of large, orange upholstered recliners that could rock back and forth while you looked out into the auditorium. Both arms on the recliners had black plastic cup holders embedded in them.

The box jutted out into space above the upper rows. The bar area was along the back wall behind the recliners. Really nothing more than a refrigerator, a coffee pot, and a wood grain Formica counter stacked with a couple bowls of pretzels, plastic cups, paper plates, and white paper napkins.

"Well, you can just tell your little friend we will definitely need more Vodka." Heidi had just cracked the top off an airline sized bottle of Smirnoff and was emptying the contents into a plastic glass full of ice cubes.

I stood a safe distance away and watched.

"You are not allowed to have any of this. The cheap beer is on the bottom shelf," she said, then brushed against me on her way to a recliner as a reminder of what I was going to miss out on. She took a seat overlooking the banked track down in the center of the auditorium floor, sipped and steamed.

I skipped the cheap stuff and grabbed a bottle of Grain Belt. I counted at least eleven more vodkas in the fridge. I twisted off the beer bottle top, and then cautiously settled into the seat next to Heidi. She had kicked her heels off, placed her feet up on the window sill, looked down at the arena, and sipped aggressively.

It looked to be a full house. A guy a couple of rows down was making his way past people standing up so he could get to his seat somewhere in the middle. His date, maybe his wife, appeared to be bitching about something. She wore a green and red hockey jersey. Based on her body language and the sneer on her face, it looked to be a long night. He looked up in our direction, studied Heidi's inner thighs spread open on the window sill for a long moment until hockey jersey glanced up at us, slapped his arm, and indicated his seat. He gave me the knowing raised eyebrows look then shook his head and sat down. We were compadres for the night.

"I never said we were going to Lionel Richie."

"You know how crazy I am about him," Heidi said, then sipped more vodka.

I knew a lot of things about Heidi. I knew about her business, her house, her car. I knew all or most of her perversions. I knew she changed her hair color almost weekly. I knew she went through men like candy. I knew her favorite foods. I knew she had a sweet tooth, was the world's worst cook and that she shouldn't drink more than two-and-a-half glasses of wine, ever. I didn't have the slightest idea she was a Lionel Richie fan.

"This isn't going to ruin our evening is it?" I asked.

"Let's just say I'm thinking of erasing this whole affair from my memory," she said, then stared at me over the rim of her plastic cup, tilted her head back and drained the last of the vodka.

"Look, to be honest, I tried to get tickets to Lionel, but they were sold out," I lied.

"Oh, really?"

"Yeah, honest," I said then leaned back and contentedly sipped my beer, feeling I was back in safe territory.

"So, the fact that you're involved in this roller derby murder, and working with the police, that doesn't have a damn thing to do with us being here. Is that right?"

I sat forward and choked on a mouthful of beer. If I felt around, I'd probably detect the thin ice I was suddenly on.

"Yeah, exactly what I figured," she said. "I don't care about Lionel Richie. I'll get the CD if I want, but don't lie to me, Dev. And don't tell me this is a special night out for us when you're probably taking me along just to provide a cover for another one of your idiotic, lame brained, stupid private eye stunts. Get me another," she said, then thrust her empty cup toward me, causing the ice cubes to rattle.

Fortunately, just as I returned with a fresh drink, the lights dimmed, and the announcer's voice came over the PA system. He sounded like the same guy I'd heard the previous week when I'd been sitting down in the Hustlers locker room.

"Oh, good Lord," Heidi said and followed up with a few more swallows of vodka.

Both teams rolled into the spotlights illuminating the center of the arena, then music started to play. It was something that sounded familiar to me, but I couldn't remember the name of the tune. The crowd roared. More than a few Union Jacks waved around the auditorium. As the noise died down, the announcer came across and said a few words about Fiona, then asked for a minute of silence. "In honor of someone who gave so much, who made the ultimate sacrifice, our darling Fiona Simmons, the one, the only, Harlotte Davidson." A number of the Hustlers hugged one another. I tried to find her, but couldn't see Emma Babe anywhere on the arena floor. I did spot Jimmy McNaughton standing off to one end, leisurely scanning the crowd.

I saw Justine, AKA Spankie, standing in the middle of the Bombshells. I could pick out Helen Killer, Maiden Bed, Brandi Manhattan and Cheatin Hart, the four teammates Justine had introduced me to at our meeting that right now seemed like a century ago.

Heidi looked over at me, glared, and gulped down the remainder of her vodka. Mercifully she didn't cause an incident during the minute of silence. After the national anthems, the place went completely dark, and then spotlights circled the track as a lone figure appearing to wear very little began to race round and round the track. The crowd became more and more frenzied as she zoomed faster and faster around the banked turns. She held orange flares or torches in such a way that made her appear to be rocket-propelled. The shadows caused by the circling spotlights made her appear almost naked.

Cheering and screaming filled the auditorium. Heidi leaned forward, suddenly fascinated. "Oh, wow, this is really cool. I had no idea. Look at her, Dev. Are those rockets? How can she even see where she's going? Who the hell is that?" Heidi said and rattled her empty plastic cup in my direction.

I sat back and watched while the woman rocketed round and round the track, going faster and faster. Flames seemed to propel the undisputed center of everyone's attention.

"Get me another, Dev," Heidi said and rattled the ice cubes in her empty cup. "Who is that?"

"Her name is Felicity Bard. She skates under the name Emma Babe," I said.

"She sure is."

"She's a lot of things."

"Jesus, she is so damn hot," Heidi said, leaping to her feet, clapping and letting off a shrill whistle with two fingers in her mouth. Apparently, I wasn't fully aware of all her perversions.

"You like her?"

"What? Oh, listen you, this night just might be salvageable. But you should get me another drink," she said, then thrust her empty glass over in my direction again, never taking her eyes off Emma Babe circling the track. "You go, girl, whoo-hoo."

She was on her fifth, or was it her sixth vodka? It was a minute or two before the intermission. Heidi was on her feet yelling and trying to whistle, along with half the auditorium. The difference was most of them weren't weaving back and forth and slurring their words.

I thought I'd spotted Manning's shiny, bald, pink head in one of the aisles about fifteen minutes ago, but I couldn't be sure. Heidi had just finished sloshing vodka all over my trousers, and by the time I got her settled down, I looked back, and the guy had disappeared.

"I need another drinky-*burp*-please," Heidi said as the lights came up in the auditorium, signaling the inter-mission. With her right hand, she thrust her empty glass toward me. She wasn't so much standing as she was leaning against the wall, using her left hand for added support. She was looking in my direction, weaving slightly, but I wasn't sure she could see me at this point. She ran her hand through her hair, pushing it over the back of her head. Then blew air up over her forehead, a sure sign of the direction the night was headed.

I knew where this was going. I'd been with her a half dozen times over the years when she'd become this intoxicated. The opportunity for any sex had passed three drinks ago. There was no point in arguing with her, just get the drink. She was beyond finishing the thing. I was in babysitting mode at this point. I'd sit back and let her pass out. Then, hoped I could get her back to the ho-tel and put her to bed.

I walked over to the bar, opened another airline bottle, and poured the vodka into her glass. I set the empty one on the counter with the others. That made seven. I opened another Grain Belt, my second, and returned to the recliner next to my charge.

She was sitting now. Her head wove from side to side. She looked like she couldn't see six inches past her nose and was currently involved in attempting to focus on the floor. I set her vodka in the cup holder of her recliner and took a sip of my beer.

The guy a few rows below us with the bitchy wife stood and looked up toward our box. He gave an understanding shake of his head, suggesting I knew his predicament, or he understood mine.

Heidi had slumped back in her recliner and let out a loud snore. I waited three or four minutes until her snoring became a solid pattern, then grabbed my Grain Belt and left the private box. Crowds were hurrying down the corridor to restrooms, the concession stands, or both. Destiny was leaning against a wall a few feet away. She stood up and came toward me as soon as she saw me.

"Is everything okay, Mr. Haskell? Do you like, need anything?" she asked.

"Everything's fine. Just going to stretch my legs for a bit, Destiny. Listen, keep an eye on our door, will you? Help yourself to anything in the box. My date just closed her eyes for a minute. She's had a long day."

"Yeah, we get a lot of that here, long days," she said, then winked her left eye. It was a little unnerving with the pound or two of metal embedded in her eyebrow.

"I'll be back shortly," I said.

Forty-two

From time to time in my life, there has been a little voice in my head that has told me what to do or not to do. I've usually ignored the voice, invariably with disastrous results. This night was no exception.

I walked down the corridor, flowing with the crowd, aware that just three stories below the locker rooms of both teams were about to empty out. The girls would line up and skate back into the arena for the second half. I thought it might be a good idea once they returned to the arena if I checked things out in the locker room. That little voice in my head told me this was very, very stupid.

None the less, five minutes later, I was downstairs, one level below the track. I was in the hallway just outside the locker room area. Overhead I could hear the roar of the crowd and the announcer's voice as the bout got underway. I waited almost ten minutes, lurking in the shadows, but there seemed to be no activity in the hallway, so I ducked into the corridor labeled '*Visitors Locker Room.*'

The last time I'd been here, some of the Hustlers clubbed me to the ground with their helmets. This was where I'd gotten into the shoving match with Emma

Babe and her boobs. I put an ear to the locker room door, strained to hear anything, which was impossible to do with the noise coming from the crowd overhead.

I knocked on the door, waited, then opened the door, knocking as I did and calling, "Hello, hello, anyone in here?"

There was nothing but the barely audible drip coming from the shower room.

I waited another moment, then stepped inside, holding the door open just in case. I repeated the process. "Hello, hello, anyone here?"

Still nothing. I quickly closed the door and began to look around. The lights were somewhat dimmed, and I had to take a moment to let my eyes adjust. That little voice went off again inside my head, asking me, *'What did I expect to find in here besides a lot of women's underwear?'* I quickly walked through the room, glancing left and right at the lockers. A number of towels were scattered over wooden benches. I rounded the corner, came in front of a locker, empty except for a black-framed, 5 X 7 photo of Fiona. A black ribbon was tied across the upper right-hand corner of the frame. A small, red vigil light flickered in front of the frame, the flame reflected off the glass. I stared at it for more than a few seconds and was about to move on when I caught something on the glass. There, smeared ever so faintly across the glass, someone had written the word 'Bitch.'

It looked like it may have been done with just a fingertip. You'd never have seen it in normal light. I picked up the frame and angled it back and forth closer to the flickering flame. The writing seemed to have a feminine quality to it. Just as I returned the frame to the shelf, there was a knock on the locker room door.

I panicked, looked around, decided against the bathroom stalls, and ran toward the door. I stepped behind it just as someone rapped on the door again, a little louder this time, and then turned the steel knob. I pressed myself against the cinder block wall as the door slowly opened, and a vaguely familiar voice called out.

"Anyone in here?"

I stopped breathing and willed myself into the wall. The door swung wide and stopped. Whoever it was took a tentative step into the room, but held the door open just like I had just a minute before, and called again. "Anyone in here? It's the head bull, the main man." The voice half laughed.

There was a long pause as he listened for any sound. I held my breath, afraid he'd hear my heart pounding, and then Security Sergeant Wayne took four quick steps and stood in front of the first locker. He reached for a large black leather purse hanging over a pair of jeans and began to rifle through it. I recognized his receding hairline crew cut and the heart shape of his fat, flat ass.

His back was to me, and I saw the creases on his neck, the fat rolling down his side, and hanging over his black tooled belt. He was thoroughly involved stuffing dollar bills and a couple of credit cards into the side pocket of his uniform trousers. The pocket was cut on the backside of the navy blue stripe that ran down his trouser leg.

I could probably make it out the door, but I'd never get out of the corridor before Sergeant Wayne would be able to catch a glimpse and identify me. That left only one option.

I had about a three-step running start before his thick head slowly rose up from rummaging around inside the purse. It was like he'd heard something but maybe wasn't quite sure. His head was up, turned about a quarter of an inch to cock an ear. He was still looking straight ahead into the locker. I was in the air after step four and slammed into Wayne full force, catching him right at the base of his neck with a blast from my elbow as I landed.

Wayne's thick forehead bounced off the edge of the upper shelf in the locker, jarring the wooden shelf loose and collapsing Wayne down onto his knees. His eyes rolled up in the back of his head, and then he slowly sank forward, like some massive garbage scow sinking beneath the waves. He hung onto the pair of jeans dangling from a hook, and then slowly pulled them on top of him as he sunk down on all fours, shoulders and head deep in the locker.

I saw his all too familiar set of handcuffs in a pouch on the back of his belt, and I unclipped the pouch and quickly pulled the cuffs out. His ankles began to move slightly as I pulled his left arm back, snapped a cuff around his pudgy wrist then locked the other end around the bottom leg of the locker.

Wayne was groaning now, his fat ass rolling from side to side. He tugged at his left arm, gently at first, but then a lot more viciously as his predicament began to filter into his pea-sized brain. I stepped back just as he fumbled for something on his belt with his right hand. I was afraid someone might have given this fool a gun and quickly grabbed whatever he was trying to reach.

A Taser was dangerous at any time, let alone in the hands of a lame brain like Sergeant Wayne, down on all fours with his three hundred pound ass pointing up at me. I stepped back a few paces, almost to the door and aimed carefully. I was a pretty decent shot, but at five feet, even Heidi passed out up in the recliner could have hit this fat target tonight.

Wayne was regaining consciousness. He groaned once or twice, then decided it was time to take control of the situation.

"What the, who? Listen, you son-of-a-bitch…whoever you are, I know you're back there. You're interfering with the law, and you're under goddamned arrest. Do you hear me? You have the right to remain—"

I'd heard enough and snapped the trigger. A coil shot out, making a rattling sound before it embedded itself into Wayne's ass. The seat of his trousers smoked before a momentary little flame appeared, then quickly died out. Wayne lurched forward and twitched a good while before collapsing. I didn't wait for him to come around. I grabbed a towel off the bench, wiped the Taser clean, then turned the purse upside down and emptied out all the contents on top of Wayne. Lipstick, compact cases, a key ring, two Tampax, a hairbrush, mascara, three or four tubes of creams, a wallet, and a lot of just junk showered down over Wayne.

I left the Taser embedded in his ass, turned off the lights, and walked out.

Forty-three

Back in the private box, I was surprised to see Heidi's silhouette up and watching the bout. She turned around and looked at me as I entered, only it wasn't her, it was Destiny. She jumped up.

"Oh, hey, you said to like help myself, you know? I didn't think you'd mind." She was holding a lite beer from the fridge.

"You can have all the stuff you want, Destiny, no problem. Did you happen to see my date anywhere?"

Destiny looked over in the corner, then pointed with a wave of her lite beer can.

"I think she's taking a nap or something."

"I think she's passed out," I said, looking at Heidi curled up in the corner of the floor. If her skirt was too short to sit down, sleeping on the floor of a private box in the Veteran's Auditorium did nothing to improve the situation.

"Yeah, I suppose. Well, I guess I better get going," Destiny said, and started to leave.

"Relax, stay here if you want. Maybe you can help me. I'm going to have to get her back to the hotel, but I don't really want to carry her over my shoulder for three blocks. Any ideas? Who's winning by the way?"

"Bombshells, they're like totally killing 'em. I can think of one way to get her back. I mean, I think it might work, maybe. But, I don't know if you'd want to like, try it."

The bout ended about fifteen minutes later. I sipped a Grain Belt, while Destiny rambled on at length about the "totally awesome concerts" she worked at the auditorium, and Heidi snored in the corner.

Once the final buzzer sounded, and the lights came up, Destiny said, "Let me go get something, and I'll like, give you a hand. Be a good idea if we wait 'til everyone is just about out of here, anyway."

"God, I really appreciate your help, Destiny. Thanks," I said, then pulled a twenty out of my pocket and handed it to her.

"Oh, wow, thanks, man. I mean, Mr. Haskell."

"Please, under the circumstances, call me Dev," I said, then glanced down at Heidi, still snoring.

"It's okay. We've all got stories of rich bitches getting shit faced around here. This is nothing. You should see some of the concert action. Once there was a couple going at it right in the middle of an Ozzie Osborn concert."

"Ozzie never seemed to have that effect on me."

"Oh, I don't know," Destiny said, and then shrugged.

She left shortly after that with the promise of returning in fifteen minutes. The teams were still in the center of the arena, talking back and forth. I sipped my Grain Belt and watched as the crowd thinned out. There seemed to be a heavier than usual police presence down on the arena floor, but I chalked it up to security for the teams under the circumstances. A few minutes later, the teams left the center of the arena and made their way to the lower level entrance and the locker rooms. They were flanked by four uniformed police officers.

A number of officers were running across the arena floor toward the lower level entrance, looking excited and talking into their radios. A paramedic team scampered across and headed down to the lower level. My guess was the Hustlers had found Sergeant Wayne.

It was closer to forty-five minutes before Destiny returned. The lights were on in the arena, the crowd was completely gone, and cleaning crews were sweeping the aisles and hauling away wrappers, beer cups, and cardboard food trays. Out in the center of the arena a crew in red shirts had begun to disassemble the banked track.

"God, really sorry it took so long, Dev. It's crazy out there," she said. She rolled in a red, two-wheeled dolly in front of her like it was an every night occurrence.

"Problem?" I said, staring at the dolly.

"Oh. My. God! I'm not sure. Everyone is totally freaked, something about a guy breaking into one of the locker rooms. Then the security jerk was involved, the cops, they had to call the paramedics. I don't know probably some reactionary nutcase. They weren't letting anyone back up here. The entire place was like, under super lockdown."

"Really?"

"Yeah, guess they're looking for someone. I told them I had to move some stuff."

"Not far from the truth," I said, hoping they weren't looking for me, specifically. "How are we going to get her out of here?" I motioned toward snore queen Heidi, curled up in the corner.

"Well, if she can't walk . . ."

"I've been here before, believe me. It's best to not wake her and just let her sleep. She can get a little violent and then, real sick."

"You mean like pukey?" she said, wrinkling her nose.

I nodded.

"Okay, well, here's what we do. We put her on this," she said.

"The dolly?" I didn't mean to sound so surprised.

"Yeah, its got a belt and everything. You can just wheel her onto the handicap elevator. Hardly anyone uses it, and it leads you right out a private side door. I'll go with you guys, in case they try and hassle you or anything."

"Gee, Destiny, can't thank you enough. Hey, do you party after work?"

"You a cop?" she asked and looked at me warily.

"No, no, nothing like that. I was thinking once we get out of here, you should come back and empty out that fridge. It's on my corporate card," I half lied, thinking that Manning and the department were going to pay so big deal. "It seems the least I could do after all your help."

"You mean it?"

"Sure, help yourself. Take it all. Happy to aid the cause."

"That is so cool." She smiled.

"Well, I suppose," I said.

Destiny expertly rolled the two-wheeled dolly into position. I had the feeling she may have done this a time or two before. I picked Heidi up, but other than snorting a few times, she had no reaction as I dragged her in front of the dolly.

"Okay, just hold her up. Yeah, that's right," Destiny said, positioning the dolly. "Now tip her forward, a little more, okay, a little more. Perfect, okay, now tip her back," she instructed. Once Heidi tipped back onto the dolly, her head lolled to one side.

"God, she's really out," I said, stepping back.

"Yeah, she's way beyond shit faced," Destiny said, then wrapped a red nylon belt around Heidi, clipped it at the side, and ratcheted the belt to hold her snuggly in place. Heidi's arms looked to be strapped to her sides.

"Here, you drive. Oh, and better grab her shoes, they look like they're worth a few bucks," Destiny said.

I stuffed the toe of her shoes into my trouser pockets. The stiletto heels hung out like little jets pointing behind me. Destiny led us down some back hallway I never knew existed, then took out a key and unlocked a security elevator.

"This is for wheelchairs and stuff?" I asked.

"Not exactly, but it'll work." She glanced at the key in her hand.

I wheeled Heidi onto the elevator. Her head lolled left and right a few times, but other than that, she didn't move. She seemed to be busy reestablishing her snoring pattern. Two levels down, and the door opened onto a dim, empty hallway.

"The exit's right back here," Destiny said.

We walked down the hallway. Only every third fluorescent ceiling light was on, casting everything in a murky, flickering light. We rounded a corner, and the door was maybe twenty feet away. A police officer was leaning against the wall, reading a newspaper and looking like he wished he was anywhere else. He straightened up as we approached.

"Here you are, sir. I hope she'll be all right. Sorry, it took so long," Destiny looked over at the officer. "Epileptic seizure," she said and smiled.

Heidi took this opportunity to mumble something completely unintelligible.

The officer nodded knowingly as he held the door open for us.

"Good night, sir, and thank you," Destiny called just before the door closed.

Forty-four

I found myself with Heidi strapped and snoring on the two-wheeled dolly. We were on a dark sidewalk that ran between the back of the Veterans Auditorium and whatever building was next to it. Six stories of brick walls on either side hadn't let sunlight penetrate down to the ground level for the past fifty years. The only illumination came from the glow off a light a half-block away out on the street.

I watched as a guy's silhouette pissed against the brick wall just a few feet from the street. He looked back in our direction as he stood there, but it was so dark he couldn't see us. After a minute, he zipped up and ran to rejoin his friends waiting out on the street.

As I wheeled Heidi toward the street, she snorted once or twice, adjusted in a futile attempt to get more comfortable, and then seemed to settle down.

"Find some bird taking the piss, and you plan to assault her later on?" A female voice came out of the dark, not at all friendly.

I jumped.

"Don't," she said and then jammed something hard into my ribs. "It wouldn't bother me at all to blow what little brains you've got all over this walkway. You douche nozzle, I thought they had you locked up?"

"Emma, lovely performance tonight," I said.

"Shut up ya tosser. You just keep walking till we're well away from this place."

"What the hell are you doing back here?"

"What part of 'shut your gob' do you not understand?"

"Just about all of it," I said, but the pistol she jammed into my ribs made her message clear.

"I'm walking, I'm walking," I said, wheeling Heidi out onto Kellogg Boulevard. The event crowd had pretty much disappeared into the surrounding pubs or cars driving home. I glanced down at Emma. She was barefoot and wore what looked like a large raincoat, very large.

"Just keep walking. Where's your car?" she said, looking around nervously and then noticed my black eyes. "She do that to you? Can't say that I blame her.

"Bad luck for you, Emma, car's at home. We taxied down. I could get a cab, I suppose, maybe, if you can find one in St. Paul."

"You'd like that, wouldn't you? Another witness that it?"

"No, just trying to get you out of here," I said, not adding *'and away from Heidi and me.'*

We walked beneath a street light. I supposed we looked like any normal couple if you discounted Emma, barefoot, holding a gun to my ribs and swimming in a raincoat large enough for the two of us. Well, and then there was Heidi, strapped to the two-wheeled dolly and snoring soundly.

"What's that in your pocket? A shoe?" Emma said, indicating my side pocket.

"Yeah, my date didn't want to wear them while she was riding on this."

"Give them to me, you plonker."

I stopped pushing Heidi, pulled the shoes out of my pocket one at a time, and tossed them on the sidewalk, switching hands to keep the dolly and Heidi upright.

Emma slipped first one foot and then the other into Heidi's shoes, rising up about six inches when she did so.

"Whoa, fecking hell," she said, taking the first step and grabbing me for a moment's support. "Okay, just keep moving," she ordered, jamming the pistol back against my ribs for renewed emphasis.

"You know, you really don't have to do that. Not like I can really run anywhere." I indicated Heidi with my head.

"You just keep moving," Emma said, but a few paces later, she pulled the pistol away and said, "Slow down, I can't keep up in these things."

I slowed my pace, and Emma walked alongside maybe a step or two behind me.

"You think of doing anything I'll shoot your bird first, and then I'll blow your bollocks off."

"No, thanks," I said.

"Zip it and keep moving, gobshite," she said.

We continued on for another block and a half until we came to the hotel.

"Well, gee, can't thank you enough for your time," I said and headed toward the hotel door.

"What the hell are you on about?"

It was almost midnight, but there was still a guy in a green top hat with a gold hatband out on the curb. He wore a matching green coat, with wide gold trim along the lapels. The coat was cut like a tux with tails. He looked like the Mad Hatter and acted the consummate professional. He didn't even blink, looking at the three of us.

"Good evening, sir, joining us tonight?" he said, then opened one of the large doors and smiled.

"This is where we're staying," I said to Emma, hoping she'd take Heidi's shoes and just keep going.

"In with you then." She raised her chin to indicate the door and followed behind me with her hand holding the pistol in the pocket of the raincoat.

"Enjoy, sir," the doorman said with a smile.

The young woman at the front desk smiled and nodded, but didn't react beyond that as if wheeling a woman through the lobby on a two-wheeled dolly was an every other night occurrence.

The elevator door opened before I could even push the button, and I wheeled Heidi inside. Emma followed behind me.

"Don't bother turning around. What floor is it?"

"Penthouse."

"Posh bastard," she said, pushing the button. The doors closed, and we rose up fifteen floors toward the penthouse. A bell chimed softly just before the doors opened onto the private penthouse hallway. Emma stepped off the elevator. She kept the pistol in the pocket of the raincoat, but clearly pointed toward Heidi and me.

"Get out here. You try anything. I'll shoot her. I swear."

Heidi gave a slight moan and snorted a little as I wheeled her off the elevator, backward.

Emma was looking left and right. The penthouse suite was the only thing in the short hallway. The elevator doors slowly closed behind us.

Forty-five

I indicated Heidi and the dolly and said, "You want to hold on here for a moment while I open the door?"

"Feck no," Emma snapped. She had just kicked Heidi's shoes off against the hallway wall and was standing a few feet away from me, decidedly shorter.

I kept one hand on the dolly and fumbled with the card, trying to open the penthouse suite door.

"Give me that thing, you halfwit," she said, indicating the card. "Wheel her back over against that far wall." She had the pistol out of her coat pocket and waved the thing to direct me.

"Just be careful with that damn shooter," I said.

"Then do as I tell ya. Leave the card by the door, then move your arse over there." She waved the pistol again.

Once she slipped the card in, it only took a half-second before the locks clicked, and she pushed the penthouse door open. She stepped inside and motioned again with the pistol to follow as she held the door.

"What do you want me to do with her?" I asked, wheeling Heidi into the center room. Emma moved around to the far side of the large table, keeping it between the two of us. There was no way I could get to her. She stole quick glances around the suite taking in the opulence.

"How's a knacker the likes of you rate this?" She waved the pistol around, indicating the suite.

I saw no point in explaining it was at city expense, due in no small part to her behind-the-scenes activity.

"Do you mind if I just put her on the bed? I'm afraid if she stays strapped to this thing much longer she might—"

"I couldn't give a toss what you do with her, but I'm going to watch. You try anything funny, the bird gets it first."

"Yeah, I remember, and you'll shoot my bollocks off, right?"

"Exactly."

I wheeled Heidi up to the bed, a king-sized four-poster. The posts were some kind of dark wood, mahogany maybe and elegantly carved from top to bottom. Heavy burgundy curtains embroidered in a gold pattern were tied back against the carved posts.

I hung on to Heidi, keeping her upright while I carefully unhooked the strap. Then I tilted the dolly slightly, and Heidi fell forward, making an "uff" sound as she belly-flopped onto the bed, arms limp at her side. I moved the dolly aside and lifted Heidi's feet onto the bed, then swung her around to position her.

"That's good enough for the likes of her," Emma said. "Untie them cords," she commanded, waving the damn pistol around, again.

While I pulled the cords from around the bed curtains, I thought of a half-dozen wise ass comments I could make. The little voice in my head said, *'Don't, just shut up, you idiot.'* Oddly, this time I listened.

Heidi had crawled into a half fetal position, face forward, head and shoulders on the bed, her ass up in the air, skirt gathered somewhere above her waist. She was unconsciously smacking her lips. Under any other circumstances, I would have enjoyed myself.

"Emma, if you want to leave, just go. I give you my word I won't call the police. I promise."

"Won't call the police? Have you any idea how badly you've fucked up the party? I thought that finger in with all your bits and pieces, and paint cans would have sealed it, but you managed to make a right proper bollocks of that. You and that straight arsed bastard, Jimmy McNaughton. The two of you got each and every one of those stupid cows to turn against me. Didn't you?'

As she talked, her eyes took on a particular glint that I didn't find all that comforting. She was back to waving the pistol around, again. She seemed to be getting more agitated, breathing heavily, her face rising in color. She wiped some spittle from her lips with the sleeve of the raincoat.

"Just go. I give you my word. I won't call anyone. Honest."

"Your word, bloody hell, your fecking word. Oh, that's rich." She laughed.

I wasn't finding anything funny.

"Climb up on that bed, next to Miss Perfect Bum, there." She waved the pistol, a little more forcefully than before. "Come on, move, you wanker," she screamed.

I climbed up onto the bed alongside Heidi.

"Wrap one of those cords around your legs. Do it," she yelled.

Heidi smacked her lips, turned her head, and gave a little sigh.

I quickly began to wrap the cord around my ankles.

"You better make it tight, so help me… you don't, and the bird gets it. I'm not fooling you," she said, then ran her pistol over the curve of Heidi's rear, never taking her eyes off me.

Heidi moved, swayed slightly from side to side, then moaned softly.

I concentrated on wrapping the cord tightly around my ankles, glanced for half a second at Emma, then began to pull the ends tight and tie a knot.

"For God's sake, she even likes it," Emma said, as Heidi gave another moan. She stepped back, pointed the pistol at me, then slapped Heidi hard, very hard, across her exposed rear. The unmistakable sound of skin slapping skin cracked through the air.

Heidi exploded, screamed, spun around on the bed, and in one fluid motion smashed a crashing fist into Emma, catching her just beneath the chin.

Emma's lower jaw snapped closed with an audible clack of her teeth, her eyes rolled up into her head, and she dropped like a lead weight to the floor.

Heidi sat still for a moment, not really seeing anything as she lurched from side to side, then she lay back down, curled into a fetal position and began to snore.

I quickly rolled over her and dropped to the floor. Emma was out cold. A trickle of blood was just beginning to seep out from the corner of her mouth. I picked her gun off the floor and hopped on top of her. I sat on her, pinning her down while I untied the drapery cord.

She moved a leg. Half raised her knee. Her head lolled slightly from side to side, and her right arm fluttered. I pulled the cord off my ankles and quickly wrapped it around Emma's, tying it securely. I took a second cord, grabbed her by the collar of her raincoat, and dragged her across the carpet over to a bedpost. I pulled her wrists behind her back, tightly wrapped the cord round and secured them to the carved bedpost. She was still groggy but coming to.

I checked Heidi. She was breathing deeply, sound asleep, just on the verge of snoring again. There was a bright scarlet hand mark on her otherwise perfect right butt cheek. I pulled her skirt down in an attempt to cover her, but it didn't really work.

"Heidi, Heidi." I shook her gently.

She gave a disagreeable groan and rolled further away. "Catch you in the morning," she slurred.

Emma was regaining consciousness. She shook her head and began to strain, grunting with her arms tied behind her back.

I took two of the drapery cords, quickly tied them together, making one long cord and then wrapped it around Emma, under her arms, securing her to the bedpost. I pulled the thing tight and knotted it behind her.

"Piss off and get away from me, you bastard. Let me go. Let me fecking go, you wanker."

"Lady, the only place you're going to is jail," I said, and then speed-dialed Aaron LaZelle on my cellphone.

He picked up just after the third ring. It was clear he'd been sound asleep.

"Lo," he groaned out and then cleared his throat. "Hell, hello."

"Aaron."

"Yeah?" More clearing of his throat.

"Dev."

"Who?"

"It's Dev, Jesus, who else would call you at this hour?"

"Did you get hauled in again?" he groaned.

"No, I didn't get hauled in again. Look, do you have Manning's number? I have something here he might like."

"What the hell are you talking about?"

I went on to briefly explain to Aaron what had happened. While we talked, I looked down at Emma. She was straining against the cords, but not getting very far.

I walked over, kicked the bottom of her foot, none too gently.

She glared up at me.

I smiled, shook my head no, and then pressed the barrel of the pistol firmly against her forehead, pushing her head back against the bedpost.

She glared but didn't do much beyond that.

"Let me call Manning," Aaron said. "I'm sure he'll appreciate bringing her in. I'll come down there, too. I'd like to see this."

"Sooner you guys get here, the better," I said.

"I'll get a squad dispatched right away. They'll be there in about ten minutes," Aaron said.

Forty-six

The Squad arrived in six minutes. Two uniforms barged through the door of the penthouse suite followed by two guys in dark green sport coats, hotel security.

"You're Haskell?" the smaller of the two uniforms asked.

He was dark-haired, brown eyes, lean. The name stitched on his shirt just above the pocket read Andretta, L. I pegged him for maybe twenty-five years old. His partner was ginger-haired, with freckles and blue eyes. I couldn't see his name. He looked to be not much more than fifteen.

"Yeah, I'm Devlin Haskell. Call me Dev please. Here, careful, it's loaded." I nodded, clicked the safety on the pistol, and handed it to Officer Andretta. He quickly walked over and set the pistol on the table.

"I took it away from her." I turned and indicated Emma glaring up at us from the floor where I'd tied her to the bedpost. Her raincoat had gradually hiked up as she'd squirmed back and forth, and the two cops plus the hotel security guys were studying her thighs, no doubt looking for weapons.

"I'm a citizen of the United Kingdom, and I demand to speak to a representative from the British Embassy now," she growled.

"Shh-hhh, please, you'll wake my date," I said, indicating Heidi in the bed. I'd gotten her situated under the covers, although she was still dressed. I wasn't sure the two officers or the security guys noticed her until I said something.

"Jesus, busy night," one of the hotel guys said under his breath.

"I called Detective Aaron LaZelle. He had you guys dispatched. I think he's on his way down here, along with Detective Manning." I was speaking to Officer Andretta.

At the mention of Manning's name, the two officers exchanged a quick glance. They didn't say anything, although it was clear they'd passed information back and forth.

"How about I call room service, have some coffee sent up? You guys hungry?" I asked.

"I think they're closed by now," one of the hotel guys said, absently glancing at his watch. He was a bit paunchy, maybe an ex-jock a couple of decades back, grey around the temples, with a couple of chins hiding the better part of the knot on his tie.

"We'll maybe make an exception," the other hotel guy said. "Under the circumstances." He was a black guy, maybe mid-forties. Not muscled in that ripped kind of way, but solid-looking, like he'd been a farm kid or done heavy construction. His nose had that particular 'S' curve, suggesting he'd been involved in animated discussions a couple of times. He seemed to have the assurance of an ex-cop or maybe a military type. Someone used to calling the shots and not having a lot of people present alternatives.

The guy who said room service might be closed was already on the phone, getting coffee sent up. "How many you think?" he asked like we were planning a party instead of arresting Emma Babe for kidnapping, waving a gun around town, and probably the murder of Fiona Simmons.

"Couple of pots, sounds like we've more coming," he said into the phone, then looked over at me.

I nodded in agreement.

"Got some doughnuts, coffee cake, sweet rolls, something like that?" Then he nodded some more in response to whatever he heard. "That'll do, sooner the better," he said and hung up.

"I want to speak to someone from the British Embassy," Emma half-shouted again from the floor, still tied up.

"Ma'am, we'll get to you in a moment. Probably the best advice I could give you for right now would be to just sit there, quietly," Andretta said.

She huffed, wiggled back and forth a couple of times, but didn't say anything else. I noticed there was a puffy swelling along her jawline and the beginnings of some discoloration where Heidi had clocked her.

I was barely into my story before Manning appeared. I was giving the long version, playing for time, starting at the very beginning. I'd barely gotten to cooling my heels in the women's locker room last week during the practice between the Hustlers and the Bombshells.

Both uniformed officers suddenly appeared very cautious in front of Manning.

He had arrived with a bit of an entourage, two more officers, one a sergeant, not Security Sergeant Wayne. The blonde female detective that had been in the interview room a while back followed the two officers. I couldn't remember her name, but Manning took care of that.

"You've already met Detective Schumacher," he said, by way of reintroduction while not giving away any details to the others. He didn't bother to introduce the two uniformed officers who'd arrived with him. He busied himself, taking a long time looking around my penthouse suite. Since his department, compliments of the SWAT team was picking up the tab, I thought that seemed okay.

Coffee arrived, along with a large tray of doughnuts and sweet rolls. Manning shot me a glance, then went for the tray without missing a beat. He took a large bite from some caramel affair and seemed to be lost in thought as he chewed.

"We were still processing the scene over at the Veteran's Auditorium, when I got LaZelle's call," he said once he swallowed. He wiped his hands on a cloth napkin, then glanced at Emma tied to the bedpost.

She seemed to think better about demanding to see someone from the embassy.

Manning studied her for a moment then turned back to the assembled group, although he seemed to be talking for my benefit.

"We were processing an incident in the locker room, the Hustlers locker room," he said and awaited my reaction.

"Really?" I acted surprised and got the distinct feeling Manning was in the process of reassessing the information he'd already compiled.

Eventually, he nodded at me, and his blue eyes seemed to bore through my thick skull.

"The girls beat up some other innocent in the hallway?" I asked, trying to move the conversation from inside the locker room.

"Something along those lines," Manning said but didn't go into any further detail. He set his coffee down and looked me in the eye. "So what you got here?"

I told him my story, starting with our walk over to the Veteran's Auditorium and Heidi suddenly becoming the world's biggest Lionel Richie fan. I left out the part about putting the tickets on the penthouse room charge. I forgot to mention my little trip down to the Hustlers locker room. I skipped shooting a Taser into Sergeant Wayne's fat ass. I didn't see any point in mentioning I told Destiny to clear out the bar in the private box.

I did mention Heidi drinking a little too much after a long, tiring day. Soft pedaled a little when it came to wheeling her out on the two-wheeled dolly. Then I launched into Emma Bitch coming out of the dark and shoving a pistol in my ribs, threatening to kill both of us and appearing desperate to get away from the Veteran's Auditorium. I told Manning that along the way, Emma dropped her line about stuffing a finger *'In with all those bits and pieces and paint cans.'*

Manning nodded, then said, "That would explain the finger from her purse, tonight in the locker room," he said, but didn't go into any further detail.

"Finger? From her purse?" I asked.

"That the dolly there?" Manning said, ignoring my question and pointing toward the red, two-wheeled dolly next to the bed. The words 'Veteran's Auditorium' were stenciled in black letters across the back.

"The red two-wheeled one, yeah. The other dolly, the one in bed, is Heidi," I joked. Manning looked at me but didn't smile. His blue eyes reverted back to lasers. Schumacher never even blinked. She just stood in the background. I couldn't tell if she was even breathing.

Manning finally nodded, glanced over at Emma, and then said to the uniformed Sergeant, "Place her under arrest, read her rights, and then put her in a holding cell. We'll move her to an interview room once we get down there."

Aaron walked in just as Manning went over and stood in front of Emma.

"Miss Bard, we're going to place you under arrest. For the moment, we're charging you with kidnapping, and I'm also tacking on use of a firearm in the commission of a crime, which makes everything a bit more serious in this state. There most likely will be more charges to follow," he said.

Emma looked as if she was going to say something, but Manning's bald head started to go crimson, and he held his hand up like he was stopping traffic.

"I'm aware you're a British citizen. We'll get in touch with the Consulate down in Chicago in the morning. Okay, Sergeant," he said, and then returned to the rest of us as the uniforms moved.

The four uniforms surrounded Emma. Andretta was on his knees, handcuffing her before he untied her. In short order she was pulled up on her feet and led out of the room. The Sergeant was reading her rights as they walked past. Her head was bowed, shoulders slumped, and she appeared a substantially paler shade than just a few moments earlier. An officer walked ahead of her, two officers held her arms, and the Sergeant followed behind. The hotel security guys walked out behind them.

"So?" Aaron asked, looking from Manning to me and then back to Manning.

Manning gave a shrug. "Look's like she might well be responsible for the death of Fiona Simmons. I just want to keep everything contained until we have an airtight case," he said.

Aaron nodded.

Manning turned to me. "We'll need a statement from you and Miss . . ." He glanced toward the four-poster bed where Heidi was snoring softly.

"Miss Bauer, Heidi Bauer. In all honesty, she's been passed out the entire time."

"But yet she somehow managed to knock Miss Bard unconscious?" Manning asked.

"Yeah, it was a reaction to being slapped on the ass."

"Slapped on the ass?" Aaron said.

"Come here," I said, and they followed me over to the bed where Heidi snored. I pulled the covers back. She seemed to react somewhat, snorted once or twice, and then went back to her rhythmic snoring. Her rear was more exposed than not, and there was the unmistakable deeper red shape of a hand, with maybe just the beginnings of purple along the edge.

"Enlightening," Manning said, then looked up at me and smiled, genuinely.

"I'm still going to need a statement from you, and Miss Bauer, possibly a photograph from her as well."

"Photograph?"

"Of her bruise." Manning smiled. "You can cover her up now, by the way. Thank you," he said.

I pulled the bed covers back over Heidi.

"All right, it's late, after two," Manning said, checking his watch. "Why don't you plan on showing up at nine-thirty tomorrow morning with Miss Bauer. We'll take your statements at that time. I'd better get down there and begin processing Miss Bard. For the record, Haskell, I appreciate your help. Nice digs," he said, looking around the suite.

"Glad I was able to help, Detective," I said and extended my hand. He took it and gave me a firm shake, then thanked Aaron for the earlier call and left with Detective Schumacher in tow.

"She ever do anything like smile or suggest she was alive and breathing?" I asked once they left.

"Who, Schuey? She's okay. She can be a lot of fun."

"Yeah, sure she can."

"All right, let me echo what Manning said. Thanks for the call. Looks like this might well get a headache or two off everyone's plate," Aaron said.

Forty-seven

I attempted to gently wake Heidi by shaking her ankle around eight-thirty the following morning.

"Ughhh, don't touch me," she groaned.

"Come on, I've got vodka and orange juice all set up for your breakfast screwdriver," I said.

It was like waiting for a fuse delay on an explosive charge. She laid there, twitched her nose once or twice, then seemed to levitate and fly into the bathroom all in one fluid motion. I pulled the door closed as she began to retch into the toilet bowl. It was a good fifteen minutes before she exited the bathroom and started to crawl back into bed. To tell the truth, she wasn't looking all that hot.

"Feeling better? Heidi, come on, don't go back to bed. We've got a nine-thirty appointment."

"You know what you can do with your nine-thirty appointment," she said, crawling across the bed.

"I've already done that, thank you. Come on, I'm not kidding. We have to be down at the police station at nine-thirty."

"The police? Now what did you do? And why do *I* have to go? Forget it. You're on your own." She was in the process of pulling the covers over her head. I came alongside and began to pull the covers back down.

"Get away from me and let me go back to sleep. I think I've got food poisoning or something. I feel like shit, my head's killing me, and I hurt my hand, somehow. God, what did you do to me?"

"Yeah, that's right, Heidi. I did something to you. Oh, wait, I forgot. It's food poisoning. Must have been the five-star-meal room service brought up last night. Come on, get up, you have to get dressed so we can go down there and make a statement, both of us."

"I. Don't. Want. To," she said, and then kicked her feet and thrashed about before she slapped my hand away, pulling the covers back over her head.

"We have to go down to the police station. Come on," I said a bit more forcefully.

"Why me?" she groaned from under the covers.

"Because, that woman with the gun, the one who kidnapped us, the woman who slapped you on the ass, the woman you punched and knocked out . . . the police arrested her. They're going to charge her, and they need our statements."

"What?" she said, and slowly pulled the covers down from over her head.

I gave her the three-minute synopsis, dwelling on her Lionel Richie rant for a moment or two.

"I can't go down there like this. God, I slept in this outfit. I need a shower, and I feel like shit. Do we have to? Why do you do these things?"

"What did I do? You're the hero here, or the heroine, and don't yell at me, Miss '*She's so damn hot.*'"

"What?"

I phoned Manning's office but didn't have to talk with him. Mercifully, I was able to leave a message that we were running an hour late and we'd be down there at ten-thirty.

It was now ten-forty, and I called to Heidi from behind the newspaper as I sat on her living room couch.

"Heidi, come on, we were supposed to be there ten minutes ago."

"You want me to go there looking like shit?" she yelled from her bedroom.

"No, you're supposed to go there on time and sign a statement. The individual they're going to charge, your hot little friend, Emma, has some rights, too, and one of them is you have to be there on time. Besides, they don't really care what you look like."

"Yeah, whatever," she said, walking into the living room looking decidedly better than the woman I'd seen with her head in the toilet bowl two hours earlier.

"Wow, amazing what a shower and a couple of aspirin can do for you. You look great."

"I feel like shit, Butthead. Did you kick me last night, you creep? I've got this enormous purple bruise on my ass. What the hell did you do? Oh, do my eyes look okay? I used some drops."

"Yeah, fine."

"You didn't even look, Dev. God, here, help me get these on, will you? I can't do it. My hand is killing me, no thanks to you," she said, then handed me a string of pearls and turned round with her back to me.

"What do you mean, no thanks to me? Yeah, that's right. I sat on you, pinned you to the ground with a funnel, and poured a fifth of vodka into you last night."

At the mention of vodka, she shuddered visibly and then stepped away as soon as I'd clasped her pearls.

"Okay, let me get a water, then let's get this over with so I can go back to bed."

Our drive down to the station was, with the exception of the radio, very quiet. We were ushered into a conference room on the fourth floor. Manning was in there, along with wild and crazy Detective Schumacher, a stack of files, and lots of reports.

"Glad you two are finally here. Have a seat," he said, not glancing up. He arranged stacks of papers, stapled various sheets together, creating more stacks and said something unintelligible to Schumacher, who responded in kind. Then he looked up.

"How are we feeling, Miss Bauer?"

"Great," Heidi said, flashing a fake smile.

He stared at her for a moment like he didn't believe her, then shrugged and shuffled some more papers.

"We're going to take a statement from you in the interview room. It's procedure, nothing to worry about. Just answer the questions to the best of your ability. Detective Schumacher here will take your statement."

Schumacher nodded slightly, indicating she was at least partially alive.

"We'll have two other officers in there with you, basically to serve as witnesses and possibly ask some questions. You have done nothing wrong here, so I don't want you to worry. We'll be recording this just as a safety measure to make sure we don't misquote you and to make sure you're protected. Okay?"

Heidi nodded yes, but I knew her well enough to see she was more than a little nervous, or maybe it was just her hangover.

"You're probably going to be done a lot sooner than me. Take my keys. You can drive back home and rest up," I said to Heidi, sliding my keys across the table.

"Okay, ladies," Manning said, then looked at Detective Schumacher.

"It's going to be a while," Manning said, once they'd left. "Do you want to grab something down in the cafeteria? I can send someone for you when it's your turn."

"Aren't you worried I could get food poisoning or something?"

"Food poisoning is probably the least of your problems down there."

"I don't know. Like I said last night, she was passed out during most of it. She . . ."

"Well, we still need to have her statement, and you'd be amazed how much people can remember once you get things going. Schumacher's pretty damn good."

"Yeah, okay, I'll get some coffee."

Actually, I got a Coke, a Panini sandwich, a piece of cherry pie, and an ice cream bar. I had just sat down, pushed my tray back, and was about to take a sip of Coke when a woman approached.

"Excuse me, are you Devlin Haskell?"

"Yes, I am, can I help you?" I said, racking my brain, trying to remember if I'd met her before, drawing a complete blank.

"Detective Manning says they're ready for you up in interview room three."

"Really? That fast? Gee, go figure. Okay, I'll just finish this stuff and be right up."

"They're kind of ready, right now," she said, clearly uncomfortable with my response.

"Okay, I'm there," I said, then wolfed down the cherry pie, picked up my sandwich, ice cream bar, Coke, and followed her out.

Forty-eight

I answered Manning's first question correctly, my name. I went on to tell my version of events, leaving out my trip down to the Hustlers' locker room and shooting a Taser into old Sergeant Wayne's fat ass.

Judging from the questions he asked, Manning seemed to be satisfied with my version of events, although he did come back a half dozen different times with something like, "So at no time did you leave your private box?"

"I left one time to use the restroom. Other than that, I remained in the box with Miss Bauer."

"Yeah, she seems unable to verify that fact."

"What kind of guy would leave a woman in that condition?" I said, and then quickly continued. "Following the derby bout, we received an escort to a handicapped exit out the rear door. As soon as we left the building, we were approached and then held at gunpoint by Felicity Bard."

Manning went on to ask details of our journey to the hotel, Heidi passed out and strapped to the two-wheeled dolly, Emma waving her pistol around. I mentioned the guy with the top hat at the front door of the hotel as well as the woman working at the front desk. Detective Schumacher made some notes. I made sure they got the part where Emma said she hid the finger in my garage. *'Amongst my bits and pieces and paint cans.'* I went on to explain how Emma was probably going to kill us. How she slapped Heidi across her ass and Heidi came alive for four seconds, knocked Emma out, and then went back to being passed out.

"Yeah, we've photographed Miss Bauer's hand and her bruise," Manning said, straight-faced.

If Schumacher took Heidi's statement in twenty minutes, it took Manning about three hours and twenty minutes to take mine. At the end of his questions, he said, "Mr. Haskell, if there is nothing else you would care to add, I appreciate your cooperation. I trust you'll remain available, should we need anything else?"

"I've nothing further to add, at this time," I said.

"State for the record this interview is concluded, at fifteen-hundred-hours-eighteen-minutes,"   Manning said, giving the twenty-four-hour time and then turning off the camera and recorder.

"Off the record, I want to thank you for your help, Haskell. Forty-eight hours from now, this woman would have been on a plane heading overseas, and we probably wouldn't have closed the thing."

"What set her off? All she had to do was sit quietly."

"There was some incident in the locker room. Your friend from the Veteran's Auditorium came across something."

"My friend?"

"The head of their security."

"Jimmy McNaughton?"

"No, your pal with the auditorium security."

"That fat guy, Sergeant Wayne?" I only had to half-feign surprise.

Manning nodded, getting up from his chair.

"What could that guy have found?"

"Another finger, as it turns out. The Hustlers returned to their locker room after the bout, and Wayne had discovered another finger in a purse. Turns out it was hers, Felicity Bard's, the purse that is," Manning said, tucking a stack of files under his arm. He gave me a look for a moment and then walked toward the door.

I stood at the table, envisioning Wayne down on all fours. He was handcuffed to the locker with his trousers still smoking from the high voltage Taser in his fat ass when I dumped out the contents of that purse all over him.

"Coming, Mr. Haskell, or have you grown fond of our interview rooms?" Manning smiled.

"Wait, she had all these fingers…I mean, why? How? Fat Wayne found it?"

Manning nodded. "Turns out she had them shipped to her. Some wigged out boyfriend packed 'em in dry ice, over-nighted the things to her."

"From England?"

"Yeah, it's why they didn't match our database. Well, one of the reasons they weren't from here."

"But still, how? Why?"

"He's some surgical intern or was. London Metro has him right now. Why? Money. I guess everyone on the team was pretty much a volunteer, except for the main fundraiser, that Simmons woman, Harlotte Davidson. She got a percentage based on her contract. Nothing wrong or illegal. The arrangement just made the Bard woman jealous, and apparently she thought she could scare the Simmons gal off and do it herself. When that didn't work, things continued to escalate to this point," he said shrugging.

"I was just thinking," I said, walking toward the door. "If perhaps Officer Trang was around, she could give me a ride home. I gave Heidi Bauer my keys," I said.

Manning nodded. "I'll see what I can do."

Forty-nine

Officer Linh Trang opened the rear passenger door of the squad car in front of the hotel and waited for me to step out.

"I don't know if that would be the smartest career move," she said.

"What can possibly happen? We're just meeting for a drink, in a very public place. We're arriving in separate vehicles, from separate locations. If it makes you feel any better, you can say we just ran into one another. You don't have to admit we were on a date. It really isn't a date, as a matter of fact."

"You're known around the department," she said, smiling, maybe.

"In a good way?"

"Depends."

"On what?"

"On who you talk to. From what I hear and saw, the last woman to go out with you was strapped to a two-wheeled dolly and got her ass slapped."

"Well, yeah but that . . . wait, from what you saw?"

She smiled wide. "Now, I suppose if I don't go out with you, you're going to threaten to expose me for being one of about fifty officers laughing at the evidence photos? A certain bruise after your lady friend was slapped across her very nice rear. "

"You mean if I threaten to tell on you, you'll meet me for a drink?"

"Okay, where?" She laughed.

I decided to sound trendy. "You know the Dew Drop?"

She nodded.

"How about eight tonight?"

"I can do that," she said.

Fifty

I hadn't been in the place since the night Carol left with that French guy Nicholas, and I met Justine. It seemed like a century ago. What passed for music here didn't start blaring until nine, and I hoped we could pound down a couple of drinks and then decide on someplace better, maybe like The Spot, or better yet my penthouse suite before it got too noisy here.

"Funny finding you at the bar," a voice said.

I turned and saw Linh, looking delicious in a short little off-white outfit. I stared, running my eyes up and down her figure.

"Linh, you look fantastic. Not that you wouldn't anyway. But wow, you really look great."

"Thanks," she said, then examined what I was wearing, jeans, and a green golf shirt with an embroidered Jameson logo. She didn't comment, but I thought she made a mental note.

"Get you something?"

"Maybe a cosmopolitan?" she said.

"Oh, 'Sex in the City' fan?" I asked, remembering what Justine had said the night I'd met her.

"Don't you just love that show? Even though it's in reruns now, I still really like it."

We stood at the bar, chatting for about ten minutes. All of a sudden, I caught Linh staring wide-eyed over my shoulder, and I turned to look.

She grabbed my arm and said, "Don't look."

"Why some old boyfriend?" I smiled.

"No, hardly, major dealer. We heard he was in town, but we could never get any confirmation. We've been looking for the guy for a month. I can't believe he's in here, out in the open. I've lost count of how many roll calls I sat through listening to what a jerk that guy is and staring at his picture up on the screen. I got a BOLO on him in my purse."

I started to turn and look.

"Don't, Dev," she said, then grabbed my arm again. This time she placed some excruciating pressure on my wrist, using just her thumb and forefinger.

"Ouch, okay, okay, man let go that really hurts."

"It's supposed to. You might do well to remember that. Now don't look over there again. I'm going to call this in," she said, taking a cellphone out of her purse. She pulled what looked like a wanted poster out, nodded at the thing as if to confirm, then dialed.

She had her back to me, phone up against her right ear, and a finger in her left as she talked.

"They should be here shortly," she said, once she hung up and turned around. "I think I've got time for another Cosmo."

"Don't you want to go strap on a Kevlar vest or something?"

"No, I don't think so. But it might be a good idea to get out of the way and move down toward the far end of the bar."

She sat sipping her Cosmo at the corner of the bar, back near the restrooms. I couldn't recall what she was talking about for the simple reason I wasn't paying any attention. I figured if things got hot, I'd just jump behind the bar, pull the fat bartender on top of me and hope for the best. Linh's cell rang about twenty minutes later. I could hear her giving directions to whoever was on the other end.

"Yeah, five tables back, in the corner. He's wearing a blue shirt, sitting with a blonde woman. She looks kind of bitchy, and she's got fake boobs. No, I'm not kidding. You can't miss them. Yeah, I thought you'd like it." She chuckled, then clicked her phone shut and reached in her purse.

"Dev, do me a favor and step back here, will you?"

"Huh?" I said, then glanced down and saw her little hand demurely wrapped around the grip of a snub pistol.

"Get your ass behind me now," she said.

I didn't need to be told a third time and moved behind her just as three SWAT officers burst in the front door. A second later, three more barged in through the back entrance. They had weapons drawn and were screaming. It seemed like déjà vu all over again for me.

"Everyone down, down," they yelled, charging into the far back corner of the Dew Drop.

"Get 'em up. Get 'em up." Yelling at the blue-shirted guy sitting at the corner table.

He had longish hair and what looked like about a three-day growth of trimmed beard, just the right amount to be cool. Some guys could pull that off. I couldn't. If I tried, it would just look like I'd been on a three-day bender.

Mr. Cool moved left, right, turned around, and then just stopped and raised his hands above his head. Linh was moving toward him in a shooter's stance with her pistol pointed directly at the guy, sexy and cat-like.

One of the SWAT guys had stepped in and was placing handcuffs on the guy, none too gently. I recognized him as the jerk who'd pulled me over the stair banister and cuffed me in my own house.

The bad guy's date was on her feet, shaking her head back and forth, screaming at the cops. "No, no, there's been some mistake. Stop this. Stop it." She was stomping her foot, then jumping up and down, screaming, "Stop, stop."

Linh had been right. The woman did have fake boobs. I recognized their bounce and her bitching, Carol. I knew it was her the moment she stomped her foot. And there, cuffed and being read his rights was my French friend, Nicholas. Pepe le Pew. I immediately thought he's guilty. He has to be guilty.

"Look, Dev, I'm sorry, but I have to go downtown. We've been looking for this guy forever. I hate to do this to you on our first date, but, well, do you understand?" As she spoke, she was shoving her snub back into her purse.

"Actually, Linh, I can't tell you how you made my day, really."

Linh turned back to watch the excitement for a moment.

"No, you don't understand. You're not listening to me…" Carol screamed, following behind the SWAT team as they led Nicholas out the door and into a squad car.

"Thanks for understanding, Dev. Gotta run, maybe later," Linh said, then reached up and kissed my cheek.

I couldn't wipe the smile off my face.

Fifty-One

The phone rang and kept ringing. After a while, I stumbled out of the four-poster bed, made my way to the end table, and the offending noise.

"Hello," I said, sitting down on the couch half wondering why room service was calling so early.

"Well, well, Mr. Haskell. I hope I woke you."

"Hey, Detective Manning, how's it going?" I said and then used my foot to shove a pair of open toed-shoes off to the side.

"Not so well."

"Oh?"

"There's the little matter of a hotel bill that came across the department's desk yesterday. Does the term city-wide budget cuts mean anything to you?"

"Hotel bill? Mine?" I picked up the little off-white garment from the coffee table and arranged it neatly over the back of the couch.

"Have you been getting spa treatments and massages every damn day?"

"Well, see . . ."

"Ordering room service morning, noon, and night, hundred dollar bottles of champagne?"

"I suppose . . ." I looked at the champagne flutes over on the large table. One of them sported a half-moon of red lipstick.

"Did you run up a tab for close to eight hundred bucks on two tickets and a fully stocked bar at the roller derby bout?"

"Yeah, I suppose, but actually that led in a way to an arrest and you guys—"

"It's eleven-fucking-o-clock, Haskell. Check out is at noon," he said and slammed down his phone.

"Who was that?" Linh asked. Her head was still underneath the pillow.

"Feel like going somewhere for lunch?"

The End

If you enjoyed <u>Bombshell</u> please tell 2-300 of your closest friends and please consider leaving a review. Since I'm indie published, your review, even if it's just a sentence or two, really helps. Thanks in advance, Mike

Don't miss the following sample of
<u>Tutti Frutti</u>.

Sneak Peek

Tutti Frutti

Second Edition

MIKE FARICY

One

She rolled on top of me, then whispered, "Dev, wake up."

"What? God, my head's killing me."

We'd met at a concert earlier that night. I smacked my lips then blinked in an attempt to come awake. I couldn't believe she wanted to go at it again. Oh well, I was game.

"Shush! Did you hear that?" she whispered, then sat up in bed and turned her head toward the bedroom door. She was naked, and the moonlight shining through the window made her white skin glow almost iridescent.

"Hear what?" I said as I tried to recall her name then clearly heard a door close downstairs.

"That. Jesus, I think it may be my husband."

"Husband?"

"Shush! Quiet.

I heard a noise that sounded like a floor creaking or worse, the tread on the stairs. She suddenly pushed me out of the king-sized bed with her feet. I went over the side, landed on the rug, and rolled under the bed just a moment before the bedroom door swung open.

"Gary," she cooed. "What time is it? I didn't expect you home until tonight."

"Drove all the way up from Saint Louis. Was outside Madison when I read your text that said you couldn't wait, and I figured, well, why the hell should we?" The voice was deep and had the slightest hint of a twang, maybe Missouri or southern Illinois.

I slithered farther under the bed and cautiously pulled my clothes on top of me just as one of his cowboy boots was kicked off in my general direction. I was still holding my breath when his jeans dropped to the floor, and he crawled into the bed where I'd been less than a minute ago.

"You've got it all warmed up for me."

"I've been dreaming about you, Baby. You were about to be a very naughty boy. Let's see if we can still make that happen."

"Oh, it's happening…"

I heard the rhythmic squeak of the box spring and her by-now familiar moaning. Then I laid there for what felt like hours, listening to his snoring. Eventually, I got the courage to quietly slink out the bedroom door, all the while afraid the pounding from my heart would wake him. I cautiously crept down the stairs and quickly made my way to the backdoor, where I pulled on my jeans, then slipped outside. I finished dressing in their driveway when I remembered my car was still parked at Charlie's, a bar about a mile away. I started walking.

I was almost to my car, in fact I could see the parking lot when it hit me, her name, Bunny. It was close to five by the time I pulled into my driveway. The sky was gray and just beginning to lighten on the horizon as the sun came up. At least it was Sunday, and I could sleep in.

TWO

I was on my second cup of coffee and staring out our office window, watching co-eds waiting for the bus. I had it down to a system. The working girls would board a bus and head east into downtown. Eight minutes later, the co-eds boarded a bus and headed west toward St. Catherine's College. In between buses, I could see who was going into The Spot bar for a liquid breakfast.

I was leering at a particularly breathtaking brunette waiting for the downtown bus when Louie opened the door. Louie Laufen is my attorney, officemate, and pal. He is also certifiable and was about an hour and a half late. He threw his laptop case on his desk, actually a picnic table, and made his way toward the coffee pot.

"You get tied up in all the trouble after that concert Saturday night? God, the riot is still on the news this morning. They had to call out the damn SWAT Team. All that looting and damage downtown, I don't get it."

"You mean the cars set on fire and battling the cops?" I asked, then set my binoculars on the window sill.

"Yeah, you didn't have any trouble, did you?"

"Yes and no. I met someone."

"Spare me the details. Hey, I got a guy coming in around eleven. Joey Cazzo, ring any bells?

"No, not really, but I'm guessing you're going to tell me."

"How about the Tutti Frutti Club?"

"Yeah, I've heard of it. One of the few bars I've never been in," I said. I was back on the binoculars, checking out a young mommy pushing a stroller down the street. She was blonde, wearing tight white shorts and a powder blue top with spaghetti straps. I was searching for tan lines.

"Hey, pervert," Louie said.

"I think she's someone I know." I was appraising her rear as she turned the corner.

"Sure she is, not that she'd ever admit knowing you. Anyway, the Tutti Frutti Club, I think the joint is owned by the D'Angelo brothers."

"Those gangster guys?" I lowered the binoculars and turned to face him.

"Allegedly," Louie said. He sat down behind his picnic table desk, put his feet up, and sipped his coffee.

"Allegedly? Sounds like you're representing them. That's heavy-duty, man. You're really scraping the bottom with those creeps."

"Alleged creeps. Actually, Cazzo represents them, or at least he thinks he does. He was disbarred awhile back, so he does the work and just needs someone with a license to file motions and shit. I'll do it strictly for cash."

"File motions and shit, is that more of your legal talk? How'd he find you?"

"We were in law school together. I think I'm one of the few people who answered his phone call. Come to think of it. I may have been the only one."

"And he's coming in here this morning?" There was no way we were going to get the place looking professional in that short time frame. Maybe we could ditch the dartboard and the empty beer case. I couldn't come up with much else we could do to spruce up the dump.

"How about if you take a hike for an hour? You know, get some fresh air. All in the interest of client confidentiality and that kind of bullshit."

"More legal talk? Yeah, sure, I suppose I can do that. We wouldn't want your client to get the wrong impression when he sees your picnic table. When do you want me out of here?"

"How about now?" Louie slurped some coffee.

"Now?"

"Yeah, now. Why? Are you working on something important?" He ran his eyes up and down, studying me. I was dressed in sandals, shorts, a St. Paul Saint's T-shirt, Summit Beer baseball cap, and still holding my binoculars.

"I suppose I could take a break from all this. Call me when you're finished. I'll be over at The Spot," I said and placed the binoculars in my open desk drawer.

"I appreciate it, Dev. We shouldn't be more than an hour or so," Louie said.

It turned out to be closer to two and a half hours. Jimmy was bartending. I'd read the newspaper, made a couple of phone calls and was nursing a beer when the bar phone rang.

"The Spot," Jimmy answered. He glanced over at me while he listened to the caller. "Yeah, he's sitting on his usual stool. I'll send him over. It's bad for business to have him in here for any length of time," he said, then hung up.

"Louie?" I asked.

"Yeah, he said it's safe for you to go back to your office. Besides, you're chasing away all our business."

I looked around the place. It was apparently a light traffic day for The Spot. There were two other guys at the bar, sitting three stools apart. Neither one had said a word during the two hours I'd been here. A regular named Rita occupied the far back booth. She was either passed out or asleep, not that there was much difference. Everyone knew that leaving her alone was the lesser of many evils.

"Yeah, I can just imagine the line forming to get in this place as soon as I leave."

"It could happen," Jimmy said, sounding hopeful.

Three

When I entered the office, Louie was seated behind my desk, counting out a large stack of twenty-dollar bills. He didn't bother to glance up. He remained focused on his task, moving his lips silently, counting each bill he peeled off. When he finished, he looked up at me with a big smile.

"You feel like grabbing dinner somewhere tonight? My treat."

"Can we get out of the car, or do we have to order at the drive-up window again?"

"I'm serious, man. I mean it, a restaurant with table cloths, fine wine, and all that shit."

"Yeah? Why, what do you want?" I asked, immediately suspicious.

"What, I can't ask a pal, the guy I share an office with, to dinner?"

"No, it's just that I have this feeling you got something up your sleeve. You know, like you're going to expect some favor."

"Dev, all I want to do is have a nice dinner with you. If it's going to be a problem, you don't have to go. That's fine. I've just come into a little bit of good luck." He glanced down at the pile of cash he'd just counted out and now neatly stacked in front of him. "I just thought it might be fun to share a bit of my good luck with you. No problem if you don't want to go."

"As long as you put it that way, okay. How 'bout the Five-Ten?" I asked.

"The joint over on Hennepin Avenue? Umm, I'm not sure they want me back there just yet. Have you ever been to Café Biaggio?"

"Yeah, and not a good idea. That's the place I took that Terry chick when we broke up. She made a scene, threw her pasta at me, and then ran out the door with the wine bottle."

Louie nodded, remembering my tale. "The Saigon?"

"Probably not. I dated one of the daughters. If she's working, she'd probably do something to our food."

We went back and forth like this for a few minutes. Wherever one suggested, the other wasn't all that welcome. I guessed it was one of the things that happened when you were an actively-dating individual, some not-so-great memories, and the occasional repercussion. Anyway, we ended up at Shamrock's because we both liked the burgers, knew most of the bartenders, and the waitresses were nice.

* * *

I was on my third or fourth Summit, enjoying the scenery strolling past us when Louie finally got around to why he was plying me with beer and burgers.

"So, what's your work schedule like?"

"I'm pretty busy from eight-thirty to about nine-fifteen every morning and maybe four-thirty until close to five-thirty every night, watching chicks get on and off the bus. Other than that, I could probably fit something in. Why?"

"Remember I mentioned the Tutti Frutti Club?"

I nodded and let my eyes follow a woman walking past our table.

"I might need you to do a little bit of checking for me on the D'Angelo brothers."

"Define checking," I said, returning my gaze to Louie.

"I'm not sure to tell you the truth. I told you Joey Cazzo was in this morning. There's just something fishy whenever he's involved. I have to file some motions for him. Everything looks okay, but I just want to be sure. I dodged that disbarment a while back, and I just don't need the state board folks taking a closer look at me."

"So, I'm still not clear what you want me to do. What am I supposed to look for?"

"Just get a feel for the place is all, the clientele, any sense of the gambling deal they're always rumored to be running."

"You mean, if I see a room with a sign that says, 'Illegal Gambling Here' I'll know something's up?

Look, if they're involved, they've been somewhat subtle about the operation for a while. Years, now that I think of it. It's always been rumored, but they've never been charged, have they?"

Louie shook his head.

"Besides, isn't one of those guys locked up? I thought he got sent away a couple of years ago."

"Yeah, that's Tommy, or is it Gino? I always get them mixed up. Anyway, the one who's not quite right, he's out on an appeal right now."

"Not quite right?"

"The guy played football as a high school kid. I think he forgot to wear his helmet. Did some boxing, I'm guessing as a middleweight. He was wounded in the service. Had a stroke a few years back that left him with some short term memory loss."

"He sounds like a medical case. He got sent to prison?"

"That's part of what Cazzo wanted to talk about. I'm gonna file an appeal on medical grounds."

"I don't know, it seems like those guys have gotten away with murder, literally, for years."

"Maybe, but we're supposed to have a little tougher burden of proof than "seems like" in our system."

"When it works," I said.

"Anyway, they got this appeal going to court."

"So, what's the worry?"

"Just a feeling I've got. If Joey Cazzo's involved, there's a good chance it ain't quite right. And then, of course, there's his clients, the D'Angelos."

"Okay, so why take the work in the first place?"

"Thirty-five hundred cash upfront," Louie said and patted the wallet in his pocket.

"Something ain't right," I said.

"Most likely. I just want to find out what it is before it hits me over the head, that's all."

Our waitress was suddenly there with our order. "Bourbon bacon chicken sandwich?"

I nodded, and she placed the basket in front of me.

"And the Nook burger with a double order of fries," she said, sliding a larger basket in front of Louie. "Anything else, gentlemen?"

"We better have two more beers," Louie said.

To be Continued...

Better grab a copy of **Tutti Frutti.** Dev ends up in the sexual clutches of a hot 'cougar' only to learn she has a sexual appetite that's way more than he can handle. The moment he takes on Swindle Lawless as his new client, bodies begin washing up on shore and they all seem to be drifting toward Dev. A disbarred attorney, gangster twin brothers, a washed up porn star, illegal gambling and a sexually aggressive 'cougar' add up to another fast paced, page turner.

Books by Mike Faricy

Crime Fiction Firsts

A boxset of the first four books in four crime fiction series:

Russian Roulette; Dev Haskell series
Welcome; Jack Dillon Dublin Tales series
Corridor Man; Corridor Man series
Reduced Ransom! Hot Shot series

The following titles comprise the Dev Haskell series:

Russian Roulette: Case 1
Mr. Swirlee: Case 2
Bite Me: Case 3
Bombshell: Case 4
Tutti Frutti: Case 5
Last Shot: Case 6
Ting-A-Ling: Case 7
Crickett: Case 8
Bulldog: Case 9
Double Trouble: Case 10
Yellow Ribbon: Case 11
Dog Gone: Case 12
Scam Man: Case 13
Foiled: Case 14
What Happens in Vegas… Case 15
Art Hound: Case 16
The Office: Case 17

Star Struck: Case 18
International Incident: Case 19
Guest From Hell: Case 20
Art Attack: Case 21
Mystery Man: Case 22
Bow-Wow Rescue: Case 23
Cold Case: Case 24
Cash Up Front: Case 25
Dream House: Case 26
Alley Katz: Case 27
The Big Gamble: Case 28
Bad to the Bone: Case 29
Silencio!: Case 30
Surprise, Surprise: Case 31
Hit & Run: Case 32
Suspect Santa: Case 33
P.I. Apprentice: Case 34

The following titles are Dev Haskell novellas:
Dollhouse
The Dance
Pixie
Fore!

Twinkle Toes
(*a Dev Haskell short story*)

The following are Dev Haskell Boxsets:
Dev Haskell Boxset 1-3

Dev Haskell Boxset 4-6
Dev Haskell Boxset 7-9
Dev Haskell Boxset 10-12
Dev Haskell Boxset 13-15
Dev Haskell Boxset 16-18
Dev Haskell Boxset 19-21
Dev Haskell Boxset 22-24
Dev Haskell Boxset 25-27
Dev Haskell Boxset 28-30
Dev Haskell Boxset 1-7
Dev Haskell Boxset 8-14
Dev Haskell Boxset 15-19
Dev Haskell Boxset 20-24
Dev Haskell Boxset 25-29

The following titles comprise the Jack Dillon Dublin Tales series:

Welcome
Jack Dillon Dublin Tale 1
Sweet Dreams
Jack Dillon Dublin Tale 2
Mirror Mirror
Jack Dillon Dublin Tale 3
Silver Bullet
Jack Dillon Dublin Tale 4
Fair City Blues
Jack Dillon Dublin Tale 5
Spade Work
Jack Dillon Dublin Tale 6

Madeline Missing
Jack Dillon Dublin Tale 7
Mistaken Identity
Jack Dillon Dublin Tale 8
Picture Perfect
Jack Dillon Dublin Tale 9
Dublin Moon
Jack Dillon Dublin Tale 10
Mystery Woman
Jack Dillon Dublin Tale 11
Second Chance
Jack Dillon Dublin Tale 12
Payback Brother
Jack Dillon Dublin Tale 13
The Heist
Jack Dillon Dublin Tale 14
Jewels To Kill For
Jack Dillon Dublin Tale 15
Retirement Scheme
Jack Dillon Dublin Tale 16

Jack Dillon Dublin Tales Boxsets:
Jack Dillon Dublin Tales 1-3
Jack Dillon Dublin Tales 4-6
Jack Dillon Dublin Tales 1-5
Jack Dillon Dublin Tales 1-7
Jack Dillon Dublin Tales 6-10

The following titles comprise the Hotshot series;
Reduced Ransom! Second Edition
Finders Keepers! Second Edition
Bankers Hours Second Edition
Chow Down Second Edition
Moonlight Dance Academy Second Edition

Irish Dukes (Fight Card Series)
written under the pseudonym Jack Tunney

The following titles comprise the Corridor Man series:
Corridor Man
Corridor Man 2: Opportunity knocks
Corridor Man 3: The Dungeon
Corridor Man 4: Dead End
Corridor Man 5: Finger
Corridor Man 6: Exit Strategy
Corridor Man 7: Trunk Music
Corridor Man 8: Birthday Boy
Corridor Man 9: Boss Man
Corridor Man 10: Bye Bye Bobby

Corridor Man novellas:
Corridor Man: Valentine
Corridor Man: Auditor
Corridor Man: Howling
Corridor Man: Spa Day

The following are Corridor Man Boxsets:
Corridor Man Boxset 1-3
Corridor Man Boxset 1-5
Corridor Man Boxset 6-9

All books are available on Amazon.com

Thank you!

Contact the author:
- Email: mikefaricyauthor@gmail.com
- Twitter: @Mikefaricybooks
- Facebook: Mike Faricy Author
- Website: http://www.mikefaricybooks.com

Published by

MJF Publishing